The Lovely Ambition

Novels by Mary Ellen Chase

THE Lovely Ambition

A NOVEL BY
Mary Ellen Chase

W · W · NORTON & COMPANY · INC · *New York*

This book is dedicated to
NORA KERSHAW CHADWICK
in admiration, and in gratitude for my life in
England, especially for Cambridge and Bury St. Edmunds

Contents

I Think Continually of Those Who Were Truly Great

I think continually of those who were truly great.
Who, from the womb, remembered the soul's history
Through corridors of light where the hours are suns,
Endless and singing. Whose lovely ambition
Was that their lips, still touched with fire,
Should tell of the spirit clothed from head to foot in song.
And who hoarded from the spring branches
The desires falling across their bodies like blossoms.

What is precious is never to forget
The delight of the blood drawn from ageless springs
Breaking through rocks in worlds before our earth;
Never to deny its pleasure in the simple morning light,
Nor its grave evening demand for love;
Never to allow gradually the traffic to smother
With noise and fog the flowering of the spirit.

Near the snow, near the sun, in the highest fields
See how those names are fêted by the waving grass,
And by the streamers of white cloud,
And whispers of wind in the listening sky;
The names of those who in their lives fought for life,
Who wore at their hearts the fire's centre.
Born of the sun they traveled a short while towards the sun,
And left the vivid air signed with their honour.

Stephen Spender

ONE · The Dream

I DREAMED last night again about Mrs. Gowan.
She was as real in my dream as she was fifty years ago in our Maine orchard. There she sat beneath the apple trees, weaving and plaiting or intertwining with bits of string and thread those absurd wreaths for our heads—for my father's and my mother's, for my sister Mary's, for my twin brother Ansie's and mine, and even for Mrs. Baxter's severe, tightly arranged hair. There she sat, telling us all in her new, intoxicating freedom about Mr. Wheeler, Mrs. Nesbit, and Charley Bright and asking my father with some anxiety about the Grace of God, more for Mrs. McCarthy's sake, she said, than for her own. Her eyes widened in exactly the way they always used to do when we in our turn told her about the Suffolk harvest fields, and when Ansie, whom she especially loved, made her see the red poppies among the waving grain.

I suppose, in point of fact, that I am beginning to write this story mainly because of these recurring dreams. I am no authority whatsoever on the nature or source of dreams and am more than willing to yield to the famous psychologists who are. Even the most harrowing anxiety nightmares may, for all I know, be closely related to one's conscious or subconscious wishes and, in spite of their hideous and often humiliating distortions, be truly interpreted as a fulfillment of one's most ardent desires, whether recognized or hidden. And yet

I am inclined to wonder, merely on the basis of experience, if certain dreams, especially as one grows older, may not conceivably be the grateful evidence of truth and reality in one's past life.

At all events, Mrs. Gowan's frequent presence in my sleep at night has prompted me to write these chapters, not only about her, but also about our life as a family in both Old England and New. She has been dead for half a century, yet in both my memory and my dreams she is still true to her merry, sometimes confused, but always resilient sense of life. Perhaps she returns to assure me of the certainties of that Other World toward which she was hastening when we knew her at nearly eighty years old, or perhaps to reassure me of the verities of this one in which we all lived with her for three brief seasons. She kept so close a vigil with me last night after my dream that, when a December snowstorm began on a rising wind just before dawn to beat against my windows, I more than half expected to hear her scratching at a pane and demanding shelter as Mr. Lockwood heard the ghost of Catherine Linton in *Wuthering Heights*.

As to our life as a family, I feel so fortunate because of it that I think it may hold some interest and perhaps even some value, at least for those who still believe that in the character of families lies our chief hope, or despair, for the redemption of this erring, perplexed, and overburdened world. Of course we, the Tillyards, can contribute little to divert, or amuse, or warn, or reassure in comparison with the immortal families, the Forsytes or the Jellybys, the Ramsays or the Bennets or the Marches. Nevertheless, it is possible that my father at least may afford something of hope. Hope was a favourite word of his, just as it was the glowing Reality which made his life.

My father never forgot Mrs. Gowan. He had often talked of her, my mother told me, when I went back to England to see her before, between, and after the two tragic World Wars. Whenever anything of especial importance to him had happened—a Danish or a Roman coin which he had dug up in his garden, baby mallards reluctantly following their mother over a slow Suffolk stream, skylarks soaring out of sight into the close February skies and endlessly singing there, the birth of lambs in a lambing meadow on a clear, cold winter night —he always wished for Mrs. Gowan to share his delight. And since the bitterness of old woes and griefs loses its sharpness with time and merges into limitless, even healing compassion, my mother, too, had come to wish for her and, like my father, to be grateful for her.

TWO · *Saintsbury, Cambridgeshire*

M*Y FATHER* was born in Suffolk, that East Anglian shire of weavers, incredible fields of buttercups, brooding, cloud-filled skies, beautiful Perpendicular churches, and small, placid rivers, the Stour, the Waveney, the Lark, and the Little Ouse. There are numberless streams, too, in addition to the rivers, gentle lines of water that seem to be flowing nowhere in particular; and there are ditches as well, which in the more level land of this undulating countryside often take the place of hedges in separating field from field. All these quiet waterways encourage the tangled growth of rose willow herb, white cow parsley, and red campion; in the early spring, primroses clothe their banks with sheets of pale gold; the red-billed moor hen and the mallard duck find homes among their reeds and sedges. So, alas! do the water rats.

My mother in frequent moments of extreme irritation attributed my father's slowness to the influence of these Suffolk streams. She came from the North of England where people in contrast are active and impatient. He always told her, however, with unfailing good nature that she was quite mistaken. People in Suffolk were slow, he said, first because of the bitter east winds which, with no considerable hills between all East Anglia and the Russian steppes to temper their force, had an inevitable way of retarding everyone in whatever he might be doing. Then, too, there was the mud, so heavy in the winter and the spring that farmers in particular were constantly delayed in all their work. The heaviest Suffolk mud is known as *slud*, a word which, he said, might well be an apt combination of *slow* and *mud*.

He was the son of a yeoman farmer, James Tillyard by name, who owned some one hundred acres of arable land between the old towns of Bury St. Edmunds and Long Melford, and not far from the village of Lavenham with its rows of timbered houses built centuries ago by the weavers. The farm had been in the freehold possession of my father's family for many generations. The house, of generous dimensions, had been framed in the late seventeenth century of stout oak timbers filled in with red brick; but so many repairs and additions had been given it through the years by so many succeeding Tillyards that its walls contained all manner of other material, plaster, flint, wattles, and a goodly supply of native clunch, that compound of chalk and small stones often seen in old East Anglian buildings and an attractive feature of many of its churches. The upper storey of the house overhung the lower; and its latticed windows, which in the summer were flung wide open to the sun and air (and to thousands of wasps as well) and in the winter were never tight enough to keep out the wind from Russia, sloped and leaned at such sharp angles and in such precarious positions that as a small child visiting my grandparents I always feared a sudden collapse of the whole superstructure. My grandfather, however, reassured me in his slow, uneven East Anglian speech.

"Nawthen," he said, meaning *nothing*, "moves oak timbers. They be for good and all."

The great old barn also was made strong with oak stanchions and rafters, some black and shining, others silvery grey and cut with narrow slits where the wood had slowly separated through the centuries. There was stone, too, in its construction

together with clunch, brick, and plaster; and some of its narrow windows were lined and even arched with cut stone like
those in a church. When years afterward I read about the
sheep-shearing barn in Hardy's *Far from the Madding Crowd*,
I remembered my grandfather's barn in Suffolk. Beyond
stretched the sheep folds and the enclosures for cattle and for
the ubiquitous Suffolk pigs, which frightened me by their size
and seeming ferocity.

When I look back upon our visits to the Suffolk farm, I remember most keenly the cold of its low bedrooms in winter
and the sound of the wind smiting their loosely fitted windows
in mighty gusts during the night. It was quite cold enough, to
be sure, in our Cambridgeshire parsonage, for the same east
winds did not spare the fens; but my mother filled stone jars
with boiling water at bedtime and, moreover, we always un-
dressed before my father's study fire, a pleasant custom which
she did not feel free to introduce into set Suffolk ways.

I remember our evening walks after tea along the drift,
which in Suffolk means a narrow lane between fields, or a
cartway given to the passage of farm carts painted blue or red
or yellow, or of cattle, or of labourers going home from work.
My grandfather's drift was bounded by high banks, which in
the spring were white with traveller's-joy and with elder.
Sometimes, when my feet grew tired from the uneven ground
or shadows began to darken the drift, my father lifted me to
his shoulders where I rode happily over the stone stiles, along
the footpath, and home.

I suppose I do not actually remember the names of my
grandfather's fields, but only think that I do because of my
father's frequent recounting of them in later years. They fas-
cinated him by their suggestions of happenings long since for-
gotten in the passage of time, perhaps even of centuries. One
was called Hangman's Field; another Lost Lena's Meadow; a

third, more happily, the Shoulder of Mutton; and a fourth, Dead Boy's Pightle.

I am sure I remember my grandmother's word for the seesaw which my father made for us in an open space among the drooping, lacy willow trees by one of the small slow streams. She called it a *teetermatawter*. The first two syllables of this odd word apparently meant rising in the air; the last two were, I gathered, descriptive of the bump experienced when one hit the ground at the end of the downward passage. Later, when we went to America, I introduced the word to the children of our Maine parish. Perhaps it still survives there.

2

My grandparents were elderly, kind, taciturn people who were intensely proud of my father, their only son and the child of their middle age, and of the advantages they had given him. Unlike most of their neighbours, they were by stout descent if not as stout desire Nonconformists, in the local term "chapel" rather than Church, being Wesleyan by inheritance. When my father had completed the village school, they sent him, however, to a public school at Bury St. Edmunds, a strictly Church foundation, where he so distinguished himself as a potential scholar that they determined to manage three years for him at Clare College in Cambridge only some thirty miles westward.

I think my father remained firm toward his Wesleyan tradition and heritage partly because he felt that he had disappointed his parents in other ways. He was clearly no farmer either by inclination or by fitness. When as a young boy he scared rooks from the fields by shaking a wooden rattle designed for that purpose, he was always conning some book and forgetting the job at hand; when he grew older and cultivated the barley or the wheat, he carried Horace or Plato in his pocket and snatched too many minutes with them at the end of the long grain rows. Once I had begun the study of Latin and Greek in the Maine academy of our transplanted home, he used to tell me of those Suffolk days and of the sea gulls from the coast swooping above his head as he stumbled unwillingly among the furrows.

There were, as a matter of fact, only two occupations in farm life which he loved. One was lambing; the other, the weekly market. He used to spend night after night in the lambing meadow when the young lambs began to come in through December and January. There he stayed in a curious small hut placed on wheels and containing, together with a tiny stove which always bore a can of milk on its black top, country nostrums in the shape of salves, oils, disinfectants, and ointments needed for the care of newly born lambs before they were strong enough to be returned to their mothers. When he heard the bleating of some ewes in labour under the rude thatched hurdles placed for their protection about the field or surmised from the jangling of their bells that they were restless in their shelters, his business was to stride with his lantern to the birthplaces, give any assistance he could to the quivering creatures, and then return to his hut with the long-legged young in his arms. To these he gave warm milk, medical or simple surgical treatment if necessary, and some warmth on blanketed heaps of straw by his fire before he carried them back to nuzzle and feed from their mothers under the winter skies. This task was so pleasing to him, partly perhaps because of its primitive association with early ages in which a goodly portion of his nature always lived, partly because he liked caring for the young and helpless, that he spared his father the night wages of a shepherd during many of his winter holidays from Cambridge.

The weekly market for the region was held in Bury St. Edmunds on Saturdays. My father as a boy, when he was not in school or often when he was, always went with my grandfather to help with the stock, carted or driven up for sale along the winding Suffolk roads, the garden produce and flowers, the lengths of wool woven by my grandmother, or the various other pieces of her handiwork in knitting or crochet. On such days from dawn till dark what bustle and commotion rent the air of that ancient town! Cattle, sheep, poultry, and pigs jostled one another, bellowed, bleated, squawked, squealed, and grunted in a hundred enclosures; farmers in worn corduroy and fustian stamped about in their heavy, mud-caked boots, caring for their animals or their garden stuff and constantly calling out the superior excellencies of both; labourers of every sort, thatchers, shepherds, hedgers, ditchers, sought to better their present wages by interchanges of confidences with one another or by judicious approaches to some prosperous farmer, known to be hiring; children screamed from mere excitement or from noisy slaps administered by tired or outraged mothers; hawkers, whose business it was to journey day by day from one market town to another, mingled with the crowds and yelled out the charms of their wares, which they bore on wide trays suspended from their shoulders or secreted in capacious bags around their waists. These included gimcracks and gewgaws of every description, cheap jewellery, brooches, beads, bangles, ribbons, hair ornaments, small tools, and toys; all manner of remedies, tinctures, liniments, cough syrups, freckle removers, toothache cures, plasters for corns and bunions, poultices for croup, salves for bee stings; and, always a popular item, fortune-telling books equally dependable, they claimed, for gentry or for common folk.

I am sure it was not the market itself which endeared Bury St. Edmunds—or Bury, as the old town was locally known—to my father. He was forever straying away from Butter

Market Hill, that slight elevation which only in East Anglia could be termed a hill at all, and going to the sloping square in front of the Angel Inn and opposite the gate of the Benedictine Abbey where he was well out of the confusion, could wander about the abbey ruins and gardens, or bend over the cases of antiquities in the nearby museum. Nor was Bury as the site of his school, for which he retained no particular affection, his lodestone. None of us, indeed, ever clearly understood why Bury St. Edmunds had so captivated my father's imagination as a boy that he was all his life to look upon it as his Earthly Paradise.

"Perhaps it's Mr. Pickwick," my brother Ansie said, when we had all returned one December evening to the parsonage after yet another day's outing to Bury and after my father had gone to talk with the shepherd in a Cambridgeshire lambing meadow beyond our garden hedge. Ansie's idea sprang, of course, from our frequent readings of Dickens and his recollection of Pickwick at the Angel Inn.

My mother said nonsense to that suggestion as she warmed up some scones and set the kettle boiling for our tea. Mr. Pickwick alone, she felt sure, could never explain my father's passion. Afterward, as we sat around the study fire in our flannel nightgowns eating scones and honey and drinking far too many cups of hot tea, she told us not to try to understand my father's love for Bury St. Edmunds. It might, of course, lie deep in Saxon history, or in the bones of St. Edmund, the Martyr, once King of East Anglia, or in the Museum of Antiquities, or in the ancient abbey ruins above the river Lark; but she was inclined to believe it lay just in the peculiar spirit or the soul of Bury, which was doubtless compounded of all these things and yet was suffused by some mysterious essence beyond them. Certain places, she said, possessed these singular spirits, which they disclosed to certain people in a strange, yet very real way and even went so far as to cast a spell over them.

I knew then, as I was to know many times afterward, that she was forestalling any irritation which we might feel against my father. When he came in an hour later, drenched from a sudden gust of rain and sleet, she helped him out of his wet clothes and made him a pot of tea all on his own, without the least suggestion that she had found the long day at Bury worn to shreds and tiresome as well. He was jubilant over twin lambs just dropped by one of the ewes and now in the shepherd's hut on a pile of straw.

"Such long legs you never saw," he told us, "and the smaller one as black as a piece of this coal."

As for me, I rather shared the hold which Bury St. Edmunds had upon my father even though I could not fathom it. I am sure my eyes were never so eager as those of Mary and Ansie when my mother fervently proposed a day at Felixstowe, where we could play upon the beach or perhaps even bathe; or among the Roman ruins at Colchester; or at Flatford Mill, where, beneath the willows of the Stour, we might well see some rare water birds; or even at Ely, so close that on extra-clear days we could see the great tower and lantern of its cathedral rising dimly above the trees on the horizon. My father was always courteous toward these suggestions and seemed amenable, though they seldom in the end influenced him. Most of our single holidays began and ended at Bury.

Once in the abbey gardens there—it was the spring when Ansie and I were ten and only a few months before our departure for America—I found among the stone ruins which marked the site of the abbot's kitchen a tiny shoe belonging without doubt to some little girl's doll. It was made of pale-blue felt and had an ankle strap decorated with a jaunty miniature rosette. It lay on the green grass among the old stones and rubble as out of place there as some silly bit of finery on someone who is dead.

"There it is," my father said. "What a symbol of the past and the present together! It's just as that dour old Scot has written in his torrent of words about Bury."

I was overjoyed by my find and fearful all the rest of the day lest its owner might be discovered. For whenever we met any women with children, my father kept asking in his slow Suffolk voice, "Has your little girl by any chance lost her dolly's shoe?" Fortunately for me no little girl claimed my treasure, and I was allowed to keep it.

When in late August we all went aboard the ship in Southampton, stumbling in a daze of unreality up the ribbed and slippery gangway, my father suddenly asked me if I had brought along that little blue shoe. He seemed relieved and pleased when I assured him that I had.

3

My mother, whose maiden name was Oldroyd, came, as I have said, from the North of England. Her father was not only sound Church, but an archdeacon in the East Riding of Yorkshire. He was a tall man with a long, thin face and long, spindly, rather bowed legs in black gaiters. He always wore a black shovel hat; and since his neck, too, was long and thin, there was a quite considerable space left vacant around his white clerical collar. He had somewhat mellow, protruding brown eyes under drooping lids, critical rather than kind eyes, and he scanned us children with them on his infrequent visits as though he were surprised that the children of a chapel parson could be in general so presentable and well-behaved as we were.

"Frankly," said my sister Mary, who loved to begin sentences with adverbs, "he gives me the creeps. Candidly, I prefer Grandfather Tillyard."

Whenever my grandfather Oldroyd came to see us, which he always carefully arranged to do in the middle of the week so that the problem of Church versus chapel should not actively arise as it would have been bound to do on Sundays, he spent a great deal of time studying the trefoiled windows and the old brasses in the chancel of our beautiful fourteenth-century parish church of St. Peter the Apostle. He saw also a great deal of the vicar, a short, round-faced, placid man, who loved antiquities of every sort and had an honest, even zealous admiration for my father. We did not in the least object to my grandfather's occupations, since they not only established his immovable Anglican position to his own satisfaction but also made him cognizant that my father was held in high regard by the vicar, a fact which he was reluctant to concede.

Up to the final weeks before my parents' marriage he had never relinquished the consuming hope (granted, of course, that he could be consumed by any hope) that his prospective son-in-law would abandon his Wesleyan adherence and read decently for Orders in the Church of England. That my father had not done so remained to him a source of both bewilderment and bitter resentment. If he had felt merely regret, my mother might have been able to share it, for she truly loved her Church inheritance and found numberless things about chapel difficult to bear; but his resentment only kindled her anger, which she was not always able or, for that matter, eager to conceal. Whenever my grandfather, perhaps in an honest attempt to lighten the heavy atmosphere in our parsonage which his presence there invariably engendered, praised us children, Mary's command of language, Ansie's knowledge of music, and my rather quick and retentive memory, she was given to a reply which, in the kindest terms, was little better than a retort.

"I'm quite sure they get everything of any distinction from

their father," she would say. "I certainly can't trace their
talents to our side of the family."

My grandmother Oldroyd was not of much help in making
their brief stays with us any easier for anyone. She was a short,
plump, talkative woman with round, calm, very blue eyes, like
my mother's in colour, but in neither shape nor expression.
She always seemed to be swathed in a lot of extra material,
her dresses pleated or gathered, smocked or flounced in an
unnecessary way and one unfortunate for her type of figure
even in an era of superfluous yardage in ladies' costumes; and
she spent a great deal of time, whether she was sitting or standing, in pinching or patting or poking or smoothing these various furbelows. Perhaps, to do her justice, she felt ill at ease.
She took cues readily from my grandfather, even stopping
her flow of talk when he began to cross and recross his long,
gaitered legs and to fidget about in his chair at teatime. She
always said, "Thank you, my dear child," whenever we passed
the crumpets or seedcake or brought her a fresh cup of tea,
a phrase which grew annoying from sheer repetition. She had
the reputation, often verbally re-established by my grandfather, of being the perfect wife for an archdeacon, since she
was never perturbed by any number of vicars or curates drop-
ping in for counsel or conferences, or by accompanying her
husband around his diocese on his tours of inspection to the
most remote Yorkshire parishes. My mother rather unreason-
ably held it against her that she "dearly loved" to teach in the
Church school, which she carefully never called Sunday or
Sabbath school after the Wesleyan manner.

4

Perhaps the marriage of my father and mother *was* a singular union, for it surely represented a combination of diverse
traits and dissimilar backgrounds. They had met in the early

eighteen-eighties at Cambridge, where they were both under-graduates, my mother at Newnham College, that recent and deeply suspected institution for the higher education of women, my father at Clare. Their romance—for it remained a romance to the end of their days together with all its ups and downs—started at the home of one of the university dons, a rugged, untidy, gruff, and most learned Yorkshireman named Bentley, who because of his eminence had been appointed to a professorship, a rare distinction even at Cambridge. Professor Bentley was a linguist, particularly in Anglo-Saxon, an historian, an archaeologist, an antiquarian, and, quite on his own, an ornithologist and a botanist. He was as well the most charming and humane of men, admired and even adored by his undergraduates. Rumour had it that he had been married in a rather soiled and tattered mackintosh in an hour snatched from his college supervisions—or seminars, in the American term; and that once the ceremony had been performed he had hastily returned to his teaching together with his bride, who was, in fact, one of his students.

During their last year at Cambridge John Tillyard, my father, and Hilda Oldroyd, my mother, who had been named for the famous and learned Abbess of Whitby in the seventh century, spent much time with the Bentleys both in the pursuit of scholarship and on various expeditions about East Anglia in search of common interests. They boated down the river toward Ely; bicycled across Newmarket Heath to Bury St. Edmunds; explored the old town of Norwich; or walked along the chalky crest of that ancient Saxon earthwork known as the Devil's Dyke, which tumbles for seven miles from the village of Reach to that of Wood Ditton, between what was a thousand years ago the fenland and the forest. My father planned all his life to write a book about the Devil's Dyke. The book was not completed, for he had a way of never actually completing his plans and projects. His hours were his sole accomplishments. He was a genius at filling and finishing each and all of those.

The Bentleys without doubt furthered my parents' love for each other if, indeed, any furtherance was necessary. They knew a great deal about the companionship of minds, for they richly experienced it with their own. I doubt if they ever worried or even thought much about the sectarian vexations and problems which might presumably arise even from the marriage of two young people so clearly congenial and so well-matched in intelligence and common interests. They themselves were deeply religious or, perhaps more accurately, spiritual by nature; yet they gave allegiance to neither Church nor chapel. They had, to be sure, both sprung from northern Wesleyan stock, which background was in itself somewhat an anomaly in Cambridge University circles around the turn of the century; but, as all know, to be "chapel" in the thriving and wealthy industrial towns of the North or of the Midlands was, and still is, quite a different matter from professing the same adherence among the small villages of the largely agricultural Eastern and Southern counties.

Just why my father clung to his Wesleyan tradition has always remained something of a mystery to me. He loved tradition, it is true, and yet he was singularly free from its hold in any number of other ways. The idea that he had disappointed his parents in becoming a university scholar rather than assuring them of the continuance of the Suffolk farm, which idea without doubt had its influence upon him, was surely not strengthened by any tangible pressure from them. When Ansie and I were nearly seven years old and Mary nine and we were all settled in our Cambridgeshire village of Saintsbury, they sold the farm and moved to a modest house on the outskirts of Cambridge where they had a few bits of land to plant and care for, a small, slow stream to enjoy, and plenty of space for gardens. They seemed very happy there. They could go to the Market Place on market days, wander along the Backs to watch the carpets of purple and yellow crocuses give place to thousands of daffodils, roam among the quadrangles of one college after another, and swell with pride over the advantages which their thrift and ambition had made possible for my father. Not for a moment did they clearly fathom the intricacies of a "double First in the Tripos" which he had achieved; but for all their lack of comprehension they were the most satisfied pair of elderly parents in all Cambridge when each June they scanned the long white degree lists on the Senate House, in a dozen other conspicuous places about the town, and even in the London *Times,* and realized how few graduates of any college had reached their son's distinction a dozen years earlier. No, one must look elsewhere than to his parents for the cause of my father's stubborn decision to spend his days as a Wesleyan parson. It is not inconceivable, indeed, that they might have welcomed an Anglican career for him in spite of the fact that they felt awkward and out of place with the Oldroyds whenever it seemed inevitable that our combined grandparents should meet together.

Nor were the Bentleys in the least influential in my father's making this singular choice of a way of life. They were, in fact, quite the opposite. Their fervent and repeatedly expressed desire had been that, after more time spent in study and research, he should teach undergraduates, lecture, perhaps even at Cambridge, or Oxford (as a second choice, of course, but a tolerable one), write learned books, live, in short, a scholar's life. There were not many young men, they knew, with my father's selfless devotion to learning; and, if they had been consulted in time, which they probably were not, they would certainly have deplored the waste of such gifts in a

Wesleyan country parish.

Had my father been of a different nature, more perhaps like my mother, he might well have stuck to his odd resolve simply to flout the archdeacon, who, once he had been apprised of the incredible, even disastrous determination of his daughter to marry a Wesleyan parson, straightway did his utmost to put a stop to such madness. But revenge of any sort was totally omitted from my father's make-up, though I have never felt entirely sure that it did not play its part in my mother's decision. She loved my father beyond a doubt, his gentleness, his quick sympathy, his enthusiasms, his simplicity, his obvious admiration for her; yet I suspect that these qualities steadily increased in value as she continued to receive vituperative and warning letters from Yorkshire. Her naturally fiery nature was only refuelled by any attack against my father; and like all girls in love she was not inclined, or perhaps even able, to look far into the future or seriously to consider consequences.

5

As I grew older and learned more about those tenets upon which various religious persuasions are based, I often wondered what part theology or practices arising from it had played in my father's mind. I am inclined to think almost no part at all. Except for long, heated, and rather humorous disputations with the vicar whenever he came for tea and perhaps also when they went fishing or pedalled off together to study some Saxon remains in a country church, I don't think he gave much thought to pure theology or cared a whit about it. He was, instead, consumed by other matters of far greater importance to him than the Thirty-nine Articles, the doctrine of the Trinity, or the Communion of Saints. As to those practices encouraged or expected by stouter Wesleyans than he, he disliked and even deplored them; and he often insisted that in this point of view he was but echoing the great John Wesley himself, who had had his fears lest the Society founded by him might lose its dignity in unrestrained emotionalism. My father suspected revivals, abhorred "love feasts," considered most extemporary prayers awkward and embarrassing, as well as an insult to the language, and, whenever he was able, avoided the use in his congregation of lilting, sentimental hymns such as "Bringing in the Sheaves." He was as negligent as he dared to be, small villages being what they were, about family prayers, partly because they were discomfiting to us all, largely because it took my mother fully an hour to recover from her irritation over them.

In the place of abstruse theological speculations and noisy indulgences in chapel practices in general, my father possessed a consuming and invincible love of God, Who, he believed, knew "no variableness neither shadow of turning" and Who had formed us all to fear Him, to worship Him, and, in so far as each was able, to work out His purposes for all men upon the earth. He was not interested in trying to prove God's existence, which, he said, was impossible and, therefore, a foolish waste of time, or in defining Him, which had been attempted not very successfully through the centuries only by human beings like ourselves. He simply staked all that he had, and was, on a tremendous gamble that God lived and moved among us and that His active concern for His world and for all His creatures was constant, invulnerable, and unfailing. When the exciting question had arisen as to a name for my brother Ansie, my father insisted on calling him Anselm after a saint, who, he claimed, had done more for his peace of mind and ways of thought and action than had any other philosopher or teacher throughout all recorded time. This St. Anselm had contended and taught that a simple belief in God would in the end bring some understanding of Him; indeed, that no understanding whatever was possible without an initial and perhaps even reckless casting aside of all one's unanswerable questions, doubts, and fears.

My father was aware to a high degree of what he always termed the "miraculous" on the earth and in the skies. He took unquenchable pleasure in watching an amber ladybird crawling up a stalk of grass, swans taking suddenly into the air, planets and constellations blazing in the heavens, ants busily at work bearing burdens twice their size. These were all wonders which he gratefully accepted together with their healing mystery.

His love of God extended quite naturally to a love and concern for all men, and especially for the humble and undistinguished among them. Candidly, to use my sister Mary's early mania for prefatory adverbs, I think that this love for just ordinary people, this faith in their limitless possibilities, was, more than any other reason, at the root of his going to Manchester, after he had left his double First at Cambridge, and studying in a seminary there for his ordination in the Wesleyan ministry. He had been deeply distressed as a schoolboy by stories of the lamentable and hideous conditions of the poor in London and in the great industrial centres, concerned as a young man with trade unionism, the warfare for the extension of the franchise, and with those social and economic reforms in which Methodism in general had been sincerely and even rampantly engaged in the second half of the nineteenth century.

He had a genius for getting inside the minds of quite simple men and women, nor did he ever assume, as did many pastors of many diverse flocks, that they had no minds to enter. He loved watching thatchers carefully spreading their yellow straw upon brown, huddled ricks, or hedgers in their canvas aprons by their solitary bonfires of the blackthorn, or holly, or beech which they had cleared away for burning. He could speak the language of shepherds and smiths, field labourers, and girls who worked at digging swedes or at milking cows in meadow bartons. Nor was he ever above using his country knowledge to help them at their tasks.

He had, of course, most trying qualities. Those few persons who at least *seem* to know where they are going are often exasperating to the many who are not at all sure concerning their journey through life. My mother used to say that, if only he would rely less on God and consider carefully his modest salary, we should all be better off in every way than we ever were. When, in fact, I recall after all this time the many things so alien and hateful to her that my mother had to put up with for the sake of my father for thirty years, both at home and in America, I still marvel at her powers of endurance, resilience, and restoration. There were, to name but a few, his annoying slowness; Bury St. Edmunds; those sometimes inescapable extemporary prayers and revivals; the problem of Ansie's school; the Plimsolls on the steamship; Mrs. Gowan and our other strange guests; and always without end the mediocre, wearisome round of life in ugly, inconvenient parsonages and in uglier chapels. My mother was lively and beautiful, whimsical and imaginative. She was made to grace other circles than those of unimportant and shabby village parishes.

She was flint to my father's sober steel, and myriads of sparks resulted when these were struck together by her anxiety or impatience. Sometimes at night in Saintsbury I awoke in my room across the narrow hall from theirs, conscious of her expostulations and even anger and of his quiet rejoinders. They made it a custom after one of these collisions of minds to creep down the stairs to the kitchen for a healing cup of tea. I am sure that the security and happiness of my English childhood owe much to Mazawattee or to the more expensive brew of

Thomas Lipton, drunk happily in the dead of night by a hastily replenished fire.

At all events I can recall few family breakfasts when quickening devotion to my father did not light up my mother's face.

6

In this mid-twentieth century it is difficult if not impossible to realize the almost impassable gulf which existed at its beginning between Church and chapel, or the condescension and disrepute which were the lot of chapelgoers, especially in distinctly rural communities in the East or South of England. These absurd humiliations had little or nothing to do with one's social and economic position as such. Dozens of labouring families in our rather remote Cambridgeshire village had been Church for untold generations. Their grubby, ill-nourished little boys sang in the choir of St. Peter's in blue cassocks and starched white Elizabethan ruffs; their weatherworn husbands and fathers, trudging to Matins at eleven o'clock in their best suits and celluloid collars, might well be sidesmen who took up the contribution, showed rare strangers to seats, and, as well, sat on the Church Council. Far more village families, indeed, were Church rather than chapel. So also were unattached household servants like our cook, Katie Lubbock.

Katie was Church to her backbone; and many of her fellow parishioners wondered why she worked for us. Her explanation was twofold. In the first place, she liked us far better than she liked "most Church folk"; and, in the second place, my mother had not the slightest objection to her laundering the vicar's surplices, for which she felt herself well-paid at sixpence each. The sight of them billowing in the wind on the clothes ropes in our back garden lent us all a bit of status perhaps; and the pennies helped to swell her slender wages, not to mention the satisfaction she felt when she saw on Sundays her starched and spotless handiwork on the vicar in the chancel.

In my English childhood you belonged to chapel usually and often only because some forebear of yours, perhaps a full century ago, had come in contact in some field or on some hillside with an evangelist who had touched his heart or made him feel sure, as Wesleyan evangelists were skilled in doing, that the Church with all her tradition and "Establishment" was not ministering to his needs as a human soul, humble perhaps in terms of this world's goods, yet dear and valuable to God Himself. Regardless of God, however, you would have been dearer and more valuable to your neighbours in villages such as ours had you been safely born, baptized, and in due course of time confirmed, married, and finally buried under the protection of the Church of England, in all that decency and quiet dignity which she bestowed upon her own. There was rarely a shred of unkindness shown you either from neighbours or from the Church; there was merely a somewhat intangible, though inescapable attitude compounded of perplexity, self-satisfaction, surprise, and at least a tinge of patronage. Surprise was perhaps the strongest element, for it seemed more than a little strange that you should be willing to bear the responsibility of your own salvation when the Church through her sacraments had been designed to arrange such matters for you, to see that all was managed in security, order, and complete decorum.

All chapelgoers were not necessarily Wesleyans. Occasionally a Baptist chapel intruded itself even upon Southern communities; and in the North there were as well Independents, or Congregationalists, and some rare Presbyterians leaking in from Scotland. In general, however, the few chapels in our region were Wesleyan, nor were we often called Methodists unless we belonged to the Primitive variety, adherence to which fifty years ago required even more social fortitude than plain Wesleyans possessed.

Few of the so-called neighbourhood or country "gentry," a word widely used in England half a century ago and by no means obsolete today, were chapelgoers. In our Cambridgeshire parish where I lived between the ages of six and ten years, there was literally not one. My father's congregation of some forty or fifty souls was formed entirely of labourers and small tradesmen, the butcher, the saddler, the cobbler, the ironmonger, a few tenant farmers, and dayworkers of several sorts. Most of these good and worthy people lived among rows of old cottages, inhabited also by their strictly Church neighbours, cottages which were set behind hedges and tiny, well-kept gardens along the single village street or along lanes leading from it. With their timbered and plastered sides and their thatched roofs such houses were undoubtedly picturesque; yet no one could be quite sure, my mother said, that beneath the thatch and around the timbers they were not the homes also of numberless other inhabitants of an active and decidedly voracious character.

7

No feat or even flight of the imagination could discover any attraction for our Wesleyan chapel in Saintsbury, Cambridgeshire. It stood just outside the village proper on the long road leading toward the open country. It was a small, square building framed of brick with stone uprights at its four sides, double oaken doors stained a dingy yellow, and a rather squat steeple of the same red brick. It was surrounded by a meagre bit of ground and enclosed by a privet hedge. My mother tried to brighten up its ground by planting a few hardy garden shrubs, hydrangea, laurustinus, lad's-love, and forsythia, but without marked success. It did not seem to welcome any such adornment.

Inside it consisted mainly of one sizable room with perhaps twelve pews of the same golden oak on either side of its one aisle, a communion rail, and a pulpit enclosure raised two or three steps above the level of the floor. Within this enclosure, behind the pulpit itself and beneath a rather depressing window of stained glass depicting Christ blessing little children, stood two straight-backed chairs. My father sat in one of these for a few minutes before the service began; the other was reserved for any rare visiting minister or for a returned Wesleyan missionary, usually, it seemed, from darkest Africa. There were no seats for any choir, which was just as well since we dealt entirely in congregational singing; but just below the pulpit platform and in front of the pews on the left side there was a small organ, or harmonium, which, considering its age, size, and general condition, was quite admirably played by Mrs. Rowley, the stout, rosy wife of the ironmonger.

To the right, off the pulpit enclosure, was a tiny room where my father donned his black gown with white neckbands which he always wore after the manner of John Wesley. The same space on the left was used in the afternoon for the infants' Sunday school. We children, together with the few others relatively of our age, held our Sunday school in the basement, a cold, cheerless room with uncomfortable chairs, dingy small windows, and a brass petroleum lamp hanging from the centre of the low ceiling. On dark autumn or winter days when there was heavy cloud or fog this lamp was lighted; but it had a sinister way of increasing rather than brightening the gloom of the room.

On Sunday mornings when the bell ringers of St. Peter the Apostle began their work upon the ropes, and the peals, clangs, and jangles sounded across the low, flat fields to mingle with those of other churches in villages not far distant, and most of our neighbours were passing through the old lych gate and over the churchyard grass toward the ancient porch, we left the parsonage, which was but a stone's throw away, and went to chapel. My father always left home a quarter of an hour ahead of us in order to prepare his mind and to get into his gown and bands. The four of us sat in the front pew on the right, since this was always set aside for the pastor's family.

I cannot say that I recall vividly any of my father's sermons during my English childhood, although I am sure he was an excellent preacher. We were taught never to take our eyes from his face, partly as an example to others, my mother said, but largely to encourage him. This polite attention was not difficult as he was always fervent and simple in whatever he said, and, unlike those of most Wesleyan parsons of that time, his sermons were never long. He looked dignified and handsome, too, in his black gown. He always placed his rather long, thin hands over the edge of the big chapel Bible on the top of the pulpit and never moved them as he spoke. Several of his flock would, I daresay, have preferred more action, even drama, in his sermons; but once they grew used to his quiet manner they seemed satisfied. Several, too, if not all, were puzzled by his prayer which always preceded the sermon, for it was far less extemporaneous, colloquial, and familiar than most chapel petitions. It was often interspersed by phrases and sentences from the Book of Common Prayer, which he admired and deeply reverenced: . . . *O God, Who art the author of peace and lover of concord, in knowledge of Whom standeth our eternal life, Whose service is perfect freedom . . . Therefore with Angels and Archangels and with all the company of heaven, we laud and magnify Thy glorious Name . . .* Whenever one of these wise borrowings occurred, I always stole a glance at my mother and saw beneath her bowed head the smile which curved her lips.

What I do most clearly and closely remember about our Sunday mornings in chapel is my brother Ansie's singing, especially when, like me, he was around nine or ten years old. In contrast to many if not most small boys, Ansie was rarely awkward or self-conscious. He was, instead, frank and friendly, sure and easy in his ways, and not often boisterous or noisy. He had a high, clear soprano voice, and he dearly loved to sing. He always stood at the end of our front pew, next the single aisle, his broad white collar glistening with starch above his short black Sunday jacket, his thick, unruly yellow hair plastered down with soapy water, his blue eyes, so like my mother's, shining with pleasure. Only infrequently, and always at the request of members of the congregation, my father allowed him to sing by himself the first verse of a hymn, "Jerusalem the Golden," perhaps, or "Ten Thousand Times Ten Thousand," for, as tenaciously as he could, my father stuck to the old, tried hymns. Once Ansie had received Mrs. Rowley's amiable nod, his voice rose and filled that bare, ugly room like motes and beams of sunlight. And it still continued to rise above the others, the cobbler's sepulchral bass, the uncertain tenors, Mrs. Rowley's robust alto, the shrill tones of the children, even after the congregation had joined in the following verses.

8

Our parsonage, although it was plain enough externally, became really a pleasant house. Like the chapel it was built of red brick and was a fairly large, boxlike structure with neither form nor age to improve it. When my mother first saw it in the autumn of 1897, she flopped down on a hideous dull-green sofa in its small drawing-room and burst into tears. She could safely give way to that luxury at the moment, for my father had gone out at once to become acquainted with his human charges and to ascertain if what looked like a lambing meadow beyond our garden was really dedicated to that purpose; and we three children, unable to cope with her distress and feeling not too far from tears ourselves, were only too glad to take ourselves out of her sight as she rather angrily ordered us to do.

Her outburst of despair, if intense, was brief. A visit of inspection from her father, the archdeacon, was imminent, she feared; and she did not want ill-concealed pity from him. Within a matter of days she had performed miracles upon the permanent Wesleyan furnishings and with the help of a few possessions of our own had completely transformed our new home. Although my father was quite manually ineffective when it came to the renovation of a house, he was only too pleased with the fresh paint and wallpaper which she put on herself with some help from willing workers in the neighbourhood. Nor did he utter more than a weak protest when a large and bad print of the Royal Family, which had dominated the drawing-room, was removed to the outlying coal shed together with a larger and worse one of Susannah Wesley patiently teaching too many of her nineteen children to read from the Book of Genesis.

"There is no woman I admire more than Susannah Wesley," my mother said, "but I can't have her reproving me every day at teatime."

Our drawing-room was an entirely different place after my mother's feverish activities were spent in its behalf. So was my father's study behind it with its books and open grate for our evening fires. The study and the dining-room opposite looked out upon the garden, which when the spring came, my father said, and he had set to work with plants and seeds, would blossom like those solitary waste places of the prophet Isaiah.

My mother deplored, on the principle of household privacy, a kitchen which faced the street, but Katie loved it since with no extra steps she could keep closely in touch with our small outside world. The five cold bedrooms upstairs were more than sufficient for our needs; indeed, my mother with her Yorkshire parents in mind or the descent upon us of an occasional missionary regretted the fifth, which was set aside as a guest-room and upon which, from pride rather than desire, she expended her many talents.

The Wesleyan housewives in Saintsbury, once they became accustomed to my mother's energy and to her strange notions about homes, which at first they said were "proper upsetting" and "fair twizzled up their insides," were vastly proud of the parsonage in its new freshness. Curiosity finally conquering shyness and even dread, they came to tea in safe twos and threes and were made to feel so much at ease that they recovered from their "twizzling" and by November were running in and out with the last of their garden produce and the best of their jellies and conserves.

"Her might as well be a vicar's wife," they confided to their Church neighbours. "Us chapel folks ain't used to a woman like she."

The thought of the Royal Family in the coal shed weighed a bit heavily on my father's mind, although he made no plea for the restoration of Susannah Wesley. One night just before Christmas, while Katie and my mother were making preparation for the waits with their carols (perhaps the single village custom in which Church and chapel happily joined), he went outside with his lantern and rescued them from their ignominious banishment. They did not, to be sure, return to the drawing-room wall, but he found a place where they could be clean and dry, as well as quite out of sight, behind his study desk.

9

It was at school that we children were most conscious of our chapel status; and this consciousness was a prolonged one since except for Christmas and Easter holidays school consumed eleven months of any given year. For us to go elsewhere, that is, to preparatory school as always the sons and often the daughters of the gentry did, would be most unwise, my father said, for children of the chapel parson, even if we could have afforded it. The free elementary school, fostered as many such schools were at that time by the Church, was our inescapable lot.

The school, which stood almost in the centre of the village and just beyond the village green, was a plain brick one-storey building of two rooms, one for the so-called infants, the other for children between eight and eleven or twelve years old. One might, of course, stay on until fourteen, the English age then for leaving school, unless one had been bright enough or possessed of sufficient means at eleven or twelve to move on to a secondary or grammar school. Near it, surrounded by a scrap of lawn and a hedge, was the schoolhouse where lived the two women who taught us, sternly perhaps but thoroughly, and doubtless as well as the unlikely human material afforded them made possible.

School began promptly at nine o'clock for us all except on Thursdays when chapelgoing children convened an hour later. On Thursday mornings the vicar appeared for his weekly drilling of his flock in the Creeds and the Collects of the Prayer Book, in Church hymns, and in stories and precepts from the Scriptures. Chapel children were not in any sense banned from these sessions; in fact, I am sure the vicar would have been glad of our presence. It merely seemed the unalterable custom that we were to arrive at ten on Thursdays.

Just before that hour we straggled along the village street, ten or twelve of us in number, and waited in the playground until the vicar, sent on his way by a lusty "Thank you, sir, good morning, sir" from his spiritual charges, emerged from the entrance. He always greeted us in a kindly, benevolent fashion, and we were quick to remember our manners toward him as the one really important personage in our little world. Then we took our places in the schoolroom, boys on one side, girls on the other, and began the long day. Vicar's Day always resulted in confusion, for an hour had already gone from our usual educational routine. On ordinary days we merely mumbled the Lord's Prayer, which was generously conceded to be the property of us all, regardless of Church or chapel, and sang a hymn.

Sums always came first. On Thursdays these were often accompanied by tragedy since, once solved in record time, they had to be copied in ink, and too many blots or smears might well result in the painful application of the mistress's cane across blundering palms and fingers. English history required the memorizing with their exact dates of all our sovereigns from William the Conqueror to our new king, Edward VII, who, though anything but a shadowy figure as he looked down at us from the wall above the teacher's desk in the spring of 1901, still seemed unreal after our long familiarity with Queen Victoria. Geography rarely strayed from the British Isles and our far-flung colonial possessions, our Empire on which the sun never set. I do not recall many references to the United States of America in either history or geography. We did learn that its eastern shores known as *New* England had been settled by some undeniably brave men and women called Pilgrims and Puritans, who had left their homeland because of mistaken ideas of their right to worship God as they chose; and we did know that we had unfortunately lost America from our Empire through a rather stupid and equally mistaken Revolution. But to most of our school America meant Red Indians, who were seemingly still occupied in a unique and gory exercise known as *scalping*. When my sister Mary denied this hotly and bolstered her denial by unwelcome information concerning the now-peaceable Indians, she did not add to her popularity. What we three children knew about the "States" we learned not in school but at home from my father's profound interest in them.

Penmanship seemingly governed most of our afternoons at school. If we wrote laborious essays, which we sometimes did, they were judged more from their outside appearance than from their content. Inkpots and long quill pens were our smudgy, postprandial lot. We copied numberless aphorisms, warnings, and Scriptural or Prayer Book passages set for us in flowing script within green, pasteboard-covered exercise books; and since our school was under the aegis of the Church, many of these quite naturally savoured of that firm Establishment: *The Glorious Company of the Apostles praise Thee . . . My soul doth magnify the Lord . . . The Holy Church throughout all the world doth acknowledge Thee.*

10

I do not think that my brother Ansie and I minded this not always tacit suggestion at school that we were outsiders so much as did my sister Mary. She was of a rebellious nature like my mother; and since she possessed a quite unusual facility in the use of language, an incendiary sense of justice, and an eager readiness for conflict, she was well equipped to maintain her own rights as well as the more halfhearted ones of the chapel children as a group. These assets were in no way diminished by the fact that she was by all odds the brightest pupil in our school.

On a morning in May in the year 1901 our ecclesiastical differences caused a memorable explosion on the school playground. This unexpected burst of fury between Church and chapel flamed toward the close of a school year which, since January, had been tense with unusual excitement. Late in that long, cold month we had solemnly elevated King Edward VII to his mother's place of honour and sadly removed the old Queen to a side wall where she looked not only out of place but aggrieved, as, one recalls, she had a way of doing, though over far more momentous matters than the religious atmosphere of our elementary school.

In any other country under the sun except England an all-enveloping and enduring sorrow over the death of any sovereign would be almost inconceivable; but to her subjects, from those on ducal estates to those in the meanest rural cottage, Queen Victoria, whose reign of sixty-four years had encompassed the life span of countless thousands, had been the symbol, even the corporeal reality of human perfection, both in her family relations and in the high concerns of State. Her virtues as a devoted wife, mother, grandmother, and great-grandmother were dwelt upon tearfully at every tea table and by every hearthstone; her stable, unquestioning religious faith was echoed and re-echoed; her picture in a hundred newspapers and magazines was studied reverently and tacked upon numberless walls; each sombre detail of her death and burial was rehearsed daily for months, together with all available bits of information about her life at Balmoral, Windsor, Osborne, and Buckingham Palace, from her pony cart to the ribbons on her bonnets, from her unmended heart over the death of her beloved consort to her dancing a polka with her great-grandson, Prince Edward. From John of Groats to the Channel a veritable orgy of grief had subdued, and vastly entertained, an entire population; and our school was a tiny but integral part in this general upset. Every child, including the smallest infants, wore mourning during the long period prescribed for that seemly observance, armbands, sashes, or neckties if black frocks and jackets were not possible. Our teachers likewise dutifully and more completely assumed that melancholy garb. In short, after four months of a cataclysmic change in history and of lesser, but more intimate changes in our emotional climate both at home and at school, we were ripe and ready for any other excitement that might present itself.

Then there was the influence of the spring upon us, which after weeks of its usual hesitancy had at last reached its fulness. The month of May is a perilous, even shattering season for the human heart in England, for nowhere else is winter quite so sullen or borne with such stoicism. Mists and heavy fog, endless days of driving rain, early darkness and late dawns, bitter winds from northern seas, sodden, dripping hedges, an all-pervading chill that reaches to the marrow of one's aching bones—these all take their toll of endurance and fortitude. In school at long last the languid and unsuccessful fires in our two small stoves were quenched for the remainder of the term. Chilblains were gone for six full months; our itching, purple elbows no longer demanded savage rubbing. The three free days at Whitsuntide, for once benign and beautiful, were over; and summer holidays were but eight weeks away. The cuckoo, already on the eve of his departure, sounded his persistent, spendthrift call from copse and spinney; may trees were masses of red or white blossom; the golden chains of the laburnum hung above the hedges or glowed in cottage gardens; the Whitsun candles of the chestnuts stood fragrant and upright upon the branches of the great trees before the parish church; buttercups filled the meadows, and kingcups, the marshes; the blackbird whistled from the tree-tops, the rooks flapped and squawked above their high, untidy nests in the elms, and the missel thrush trilled and warbled for hours on end among the garden shrubs. With all this madness without, we squirmed on our hard benches within, hated our teachers, thought only of gathering cowslips, feeding swans, fishing in every stream, and playing cricket in the long, bright evenings.

I do not, of course, lay the responsibility for my sister Mary's disgraceful conduct in the school playground either upon the death of the old Queen or upon the spring; yet each had indirectly done its part in engendering the restlessness which goaded her and which quivered within us all. The direct cause of outbreak was St. Peter the Apostle, whose day fell on June 29. Since he was the patron saint of our parish church, this date was always celebrated by an early-morning service and later in the day by a village fête or festival, to which chapel folks were always welcome but in which they usually took no active part since all arrangements for it were made by the vicar, his sidesmen, his teachers, his council, his church-wardens, and his choir.

Our headmistress and the teacher of our room, Miss Caxton, doubtless beside herself from the general feverishness with which she had to cope and longing for a change from the usual turgid round of sums and history, announced on this fatal morning a surprise for the vicar as well as a contest for us. We were all to copy in our best script the Collect for St. Peter's Day, or even to print it in fine block letters if we felt sure enough of our talents to do so. She promised that she would place the best copy in a frame so that the vicar might actually read from it as he stood at the altar in the early morning. In further desperation she overwhelmed us all by offering a prize of half a crown for the winning production.

We were not at all averse to escaping our usual dull routine; and the very notion of half a crown, which meant affluence beyond description, fired us to unprecedented zeal. For two hours we dipped and scratched as we strove to fit the collect upon the single sheet of lined paper. Meanwhile Miss Caxton, giving herself up gladly to the spring, gazed from our murky windows in more peace than she had known for months.

At promptly eleven o'clock, the time for playground games and exercise, our creations were demanded and brought to Miss Caxton's desk, from which they were propped against the blackboard for the judgement of us all. In this judgement Miss Hawes, the infants' teacher, joined, bringing along her twelve infants, who, although they were allowed no power of choice, gazed with awe upon the results of our corporate genius. These ranged widely both in quality of work and in cleanliness. Some bore smudges, blots, and misspellings; others were incomplete; several scribes had failed in apportioning the necessary words to the space allotted them. My own copy was clearly a mess since I had too lavishly filled my pen for both "God" and "Bishops" with awful results; and Ansie's was little better, for he at the very start had put an extra *l* in "Almighty," which, he told me later, had so unnerved him that all the following words trembled on his paper.

Actually no formal judgement was necessary. Common consent prevailed. Mary's copy stood so above all the others that with one reluctant accord we awarded her signal honour and half a crown. She had printed the Collect in really beautiful block letters and had so carefully arranged her spacing that the "Amen" was quite alone by itself on the next to the lowest line. There was not the faintest suggestion of a smear, let alone a blot or a smudge. Her clear black lettering on the clean white paper was a triumph both of extreme care and, in our inexperienced eyes, of distinguished talent.

Her cheeks grew very red as she walked forward amid applause to receive her prize. It was a trifle disappointing, to be sure, to be given a shilling and three rather tarnished sixpences instead of the big, round piece of silver itself. Miss Caxton had obviously conceived the contest on the spur of a dishearten-ing moment and had left home unprepared in proper coinage. Still, though thus dismantled, it *was* half a crown.

When the winner had returned to her bench, which she shared with Susan Pratt, the daughter of the proprietor of our one public house, The Green Man, and Miss Hawes had de-parted with the impressed infants to her side of the partition which separated our two rooms, yet another triumph followed for my sister.

"I think it might be helpful for us all," Miss Caxton said, standing at her desk in her worn grey dress with her pale-grey eyes blinking behind her gold-rimmed spectacles, "if Mary would tell us just how she went about her work to produce so splendid a result."

Mary rose to her feet amid wiggling and scuffling, for we were eager to get out into the playground. With all her dis-tinction and the four coins in the pocket of her pinafore, she was modest in her explanation.

"I counted the words first," she said, "so that I'd know how many to put on each line. The Collect has sixty-three words, and there were twelve lines on the paper. So I just reckoned as well as I could with the short words and the long ones. I thought it would be nice if I could save one line just for the 'Amen' by itself."

"Admirable," Miss Caxton said. "I'm sure we can all profit from Mary's care before she even began to copy. I know the vicar will be delighted; and you can all see the Collect in its nice frame on the altar on St. Peter's Day."

Her final statement was, of course, unfortunate, but it might well have passed unnoticed had it not been for Susan Pratt.

Susan's resentment of Mary's success was deepened both by
daily proximity with a seatmate brighter than she and by the
recognition that her own copy was indescribably bad, and un-
finished as well. Her resentment, of course, might have been
fed by the Collect itself, which, as all familiar with the Book
of Common Prayer know, is somewhat more closely tied than
others to the Church in view of the fact that St. Peter had been
declared its foundation. It is doubtful, however, that Susan was
intelligent enough to be bolstered by that knowledge. Now,
to our collective amazement, she rose to her feet, without even
raising her hand for permission, and faced Miss Caxton.

"Her won't see it," she said, "because her's chapel. I think
myself, miss, the 'alf a crown belongs to a proper Churchgoer.
Chapel folks knows nothin' about collects or saints."

The silence which followed Susan's remarks was ominous.
We were all so stunned that we ceased our hitching about. It
was incredible that a schoolmistress could be thus taken to
task and especially by so soggy and stupid a child as Susan
Pratt with her short, fat legs and her stringy hair.

Miss Caxton, taken aback though she was, rallied well.

"That will do, Susan," she said sharply. "The contest had
nothing to do with Church or chapel. Please sit down. Now,
children, playtime, and remember your manners in the future."

We all rushed for the door and the healing sunlight. Miss
Caxton and Miss Hawes, instead of deciding which should remain with us for purposes of supervision as was their custom,
started for the schoolhouse to make a calming cup of tea. They
looked as though they were in huddled, outraged confidence
as they moved toward the opening in the hedge.

Susan's round, rather flat face was crimson and her eyes
were blazing. With her Whitsuntide Confirmation by the great
Bishop of Ely himself in his mitre and his embroidered robes
doubtless lending her courage, she dragged Mary, who was

not in the least disposed to resist her, toward the corner of
the playground farthest from the schoolhouse. I am sure that
Mary had not imagined actual physical combat. Perhaps she
had relied upon her superiority over Susan in the use of words.
She recovered herself quickly, however, once she realized the
nature of the onslaught, but not before Susan had dealt a telling blow upon her nose with her right fist which was instantly
followed by some scratchings on her face. Then, injustice
blazing within her and all seemliness cast to the winds, she
sprung into delayed, but vigorous action. She was taller and
more agile than Susan, and in a matter of minutes or even
seconds she had mauled her antagonist's face in generous return
and so expertly managed a tripping movement upon one of her
legs that Susan was screaming and writhing on the gravel of
the playground.

As onlookers the thirty or so of their schoolmates were
quite useless. We were all too horrified to intervene or to
range ourselves on one side or the other in terms of loyalty.
Even the older boys did nothing but cry "Coo!" in amazement
as they witnessed the brief conflict. Two infants ran bawling
toward the schoolhouse. Our teachers lost no time in reaching
the scene. Both combatants were summarily sent to their
homes; Miss Hawes gathered the terrified infants together and
administered pacifying sweets; Miss Caxton herded the others
of us inside, where we were too subdued and cowed even to
listen to her furious upbraidings.

I caught a glimpse of Mary as she moved homeward down
the village street. I must confess to a measure of admiration
for her because she carried her head and shoulders high, although the blood flowing from her nose required constant
and rather undignified attention. Ansie was clearly crushed.
He kept stealing desperate glances at me from his side of
our room, and I could see that he was striving to keep back his

tears.

The aftermath of this event has perhaps remained with me in more concrete detail than the event itself. In the early evening Mr. Pratt came down our road from The Green Man leading his daughter by the hand. He was a tall, large, rather shambling man with a kind, florid face. He had dressed up for the occasion in his black suit and a stiff white collar with a black bow tie set a bit crookedly upon the collar stud. Susan was in a clean pink frock, an ill-chosen colour since one of her eyes was completely sealed by a deep purple lump, the size and hue of an Easter egg. She looked bedraggled and miserable as they neared our hedge. My mother's heart warmed toward her, and she hastily asked Katie to get together some biscuits and some lemon squash.

My father went out to meet them while we children in acute embarrassment waited in the doorway for their entrance. Mr. Pratt was a solid though quite passionless Churchman; and my father and he were friends. He was too bald at the top of his head to have any hair to pull after the country manner; but he carefully touched his forehead, together with removing his hat.

"I'm 'ere to apologize, sir," he said while Susan sniffled in her handkerchief. "I don't holds with such goin's-on, nor do me wife. All this ol' nonsense ower Church nor chapel ain't nothin' to me. I serves both an' looks on both equal long's them pay their reckonin's. Susan, speak yer piece."

"I'm sorry," mumbled Susan from her dripping handkerchief.

"More, me girl," her father said sternly. "That ain't all you was to say."

"That's quite enough, Susan," my mother said, for she had now joined my father at the hedge. "Please don't make her say any more, Mr. Pratt. Mary is sorry, too. She behaved very

badly, and we're all ashamed. It's quite too silly for us to remember. Let's go into the garden for a nice talk."

Mr. Pratt held his ground.

"Sorry, ma'am," he said, "but her has to say it all. Her mum's
waitin' at 'ome to hear. Now, Susan, the finish."

"I didn't ought to do it," managed Susan. "Twan't right, an'
I knows it now. I've brung Mary my best marble. No one tol'
me to do it, neither."

The visit in our garden was not too successful as a purely
social affair. My father and Mr. Pratt sat by a table and drank
some ale which my mother brought them. My father thought
a pipe each would help out matters and fetched Mr. Pratt a
fresh clay one from his study since Mr. Pratt had left his at
home. They talked about the weather; the prospects for an
early harvest; the incalculable loss to England of the old
Queen; and how only a first-class thatcher could make cross-
pieces and braids on ricks and roofs. Mary and Susan sat a
short distance away, gurgling lemon squash and munching
biscuits, saying nothing. The marble was a large and beautiful
one of transparent glass with a tiny white bear ingeniously
placed inside. I felt sorry for Susan's sacrifice and thought
that Mary had done rather well for herself, what with the
marble and half a crown. The late sun still shone brightly, and
the cries of some boys at cricket drifted back from a nearby
field. Ansie and I soon escaped to the back garden where we
aimlessly knocked some croquet balls about.

Sometime in the night I awoke in the bed which I shared
with Mary to hear her sobbing into her pillow. Then I knew
that she was wretched, beyond any cure from a marble, half
a crown, or even victory in battle. I ached to comfort her,
but I said nothing at all. For I suddenly understood in that
clear perception sometimes granted to children that her sorrow was too deep for any shallow comfort of mine. It went

far back, quite out of sight for both her and me, to those days in Suffolk when my father, following the furrows, had made up his stubborn mind to stick closely to John Wesley, whatever the heavy cost.

11

If this unfortunate episode had occurred a year or even several months earlier, it might have exerted some slight influence on our decision to go, or, as my father invariably said, to *emigrate* to America; but, as it happened, our plans were already nearing completion. For several years there had been strong motives for emigration at work in my father's mind, among which were his new literary enthusiasms, his exalted conception of American democracy, and the problem of Ansie's school. Of all these the last-named was the first in importance.

In England at the turn of the present century the question of a school for a young boy was perhaps the weightiest question to be answered, at least among families which were determined, for social or educational reasons, upon a good school for their sons; and even today it still engages and requires a great deal of attention. Then it made little difference whether or not a boy went on to the Universities; but his parents' choice of a school for him was of primary and vital importance to his future well-being and happiness, even to his success in life. In our family it seemed, at least to Mary and me, as though our parents talked about little else during our four years in Saintsbury except about what should be done with Ansie. Mere girls did not matter so much in those days. If they were extraordinarily bright and promising, they might, given daring and emancipated parents, dream of the still-new colleges for women at Oxford and Cambridge after some years at boarding school. If they were only average and pleasant girls, they remained at home after seventeen or eighteen, contributing to the enjoyment and comfort of their families until marriage mercifully rescued them; or, if they did not marry, they might be sure that in course of time they could spend the rest of their lives in looking after one or two aged parents. The problem of Mary and me, therefore, although it may have existed in some dim recesses of my parents' minds, was as nothing in comparison with their concern over Ansie; and as we approached our tenth birthday, an age when many boys were already in preparatory schools with "public" ones but three or four years away, this problem increased to enormous size and weight. To it was firmly attached beyond any hope of severance the added problem of pounds, shillings, and pence.

The solution of a school for Ansie might have been easier could it have been confined to our own immediate family, but that seemed impossible. First of all the vicar (whose name was Mr. Read though some of the more "advanced" among the gentry in his flock called him "Father," to his discomfiture, since he was quite safely Low Church) intruded himself into our deliberations. Because of Ansie's voice and his ability to read even difficult music, Mr. Read wanted him to try for the King's College choir in nearby Cambridge. He felt quite sure, he said, that Ansie would win out there, and, if he did, he would be assured of a practically free education at the Choir School in return for his singing in King's College Chapel. The vicar further generously declared that it didn't make a whit of difference, or wouldn't with *his* backing, whether Ansie stemmed from Church or chapel. All that mattered was his voice.

Mary and I loved to think of Ansie in the King's Choir School. Once there he would wear grey knee socks with a band of purple, a purple jacket, and a black cap with a white fleur-de-lis on it. In the great, dim chapel he would sing in a red cassock, his high clear soprano echoing among the vaulting, fan-shaped arches of the fifteenth-century ceiling.

" 'Music lingering on as loth to die,' " my father said, quoting Wordsworth, and yet he was disinclined toward the Choir School for Ansie. He thought, and perhaps with good reason, that such a solution of Ansie's problem would be unwise, and even far-reaching in its consequences, in view of his own position in Saintsbury. My mother tolerantly voiced no opinion on this matter, although I am sure that, like Mary and me, she had her exciting moments of seeing Ansie in his purple school coat or in his red cassock.

She was, however, not at all silent when her father, the archdeacon, offered his advice as to Ansie's education. He made several visits to our parsonage to discuss it and wrote numberless letters as well. It was his well-considered opinion, he said, both orally and in writing, that Ansie should come to Yorkshire. There in ancient King Edwin's School at York, which dated as far back as the days of Alcuin in the eighth century, Ansie might be assured of a most superior training in the Classics and, he felt sure, be granted as well the inestimable privilege of singing in York Minster. He would be assured, too, of a real home with his grandparents during his briefer holidays. Finally, as my grandfather's most telling inducement, he offered to bear all expenses for Ansie at King Edwin's School.

My father was understandably hesitant in view of this overwhelming generosity in the matter of fees, for with Ansie's future at stake he was willing to set aside his stalwart pride; but my mother was as immovable as God Himself.

"He can go to any grammar school in England," she said to my father one day upon the receipt of a rather peremptory letter from the archdeacon. "Or he can stay right here with Miss Caxton until he's fourteen. He shall never go to Yorkshire. Now that's that, and there's an end of it."

Even Katie had had her say about Yorkshire. One evening, following a visit from my grandfather Oldroyd, when she was giving Ansie and me some teacake in the kitchen after we had been playing late at jackstones in the garden, she put her arms akimbo and glared at us both as we perched on her clean table.

"I hope I knows me place," she said, "but I can't thole York for you, me boy. Namin' no names, of course, York would be a fair awful place for the likes o' you. You crawl right under your mum's wings, who knows what's what about that school up north, old though it may be."

In all this confusion and indecision Ansie felt, he said, like some cricket ball with half the stuffing out being batted unmercifully about; but after my mother's ultimatum he took heart, at least about York. He had dreamed one night that he was singing in the Minster when, catching sight of the archdeacon in one of the high chancel stalls, he lost all control of his voice which went off into so many forbidden flats and sharps that he was dragged from the choir by the hair of his head in the outraged hands of the choirmaster. When he told his dream at breakfast, my mother gave my father such a look that he left the table. We were finally convinced then that the awful spectre of King Edwin's School was "laid and staked," in Katie's words, for good and would never rise again.

My father meanwhile had been doing a good bit of reading about American schools, and we all, of course, shared his researches into them.

"It seems that there are these academies in the towns and even small villages all over the States," he said. "In some districts they favour the term 'high school.' 'Academy,' I take it, is used mostly in New England. They are free schools, too— anyone can go to them; in fact, most boys, and girls too, do go. They are prepared for college there, and they can live at home with their parents. Can you imagine it, my dear?"

"I can imagine anything after thirteen years with you," my mother said. But she said it merrily, and she kissed my father before she gathered up her trappings for an unwelcome jumble sale to help swell the meagre resources of the Chapel Women's Fund.

12

When my father was not viewing, or hunting for, antiquities, with or without the vicar, or talking over back fences with his parishioners, or spending winter hours in the lambing meadow with the shepherd, or pottering about our garden, or journeying to Bury St. Edmunds, he was reading. Like most men of his make-up he found in books men of larger stature than he found in life outside them, not to mention the thoughts he discovered there. He was inclined, like many avid readers, to be consumed with one passion for a season before the next claimed his mind and heart. During our years in Saintsbury, perhaps from the idea of America sitting uneasily in his consciousness or actively nagging at him, he eagerly surrendered himself to two writers, Alexis de Tocqueville and Henry David Thoreau.

When we pooled our combined resources to give him *Democracy in America* on his thirty-eighth birthday, he was so overcome with delight at the two fat volumes which he could now mark up as he liked that he paid scant attention to Katie's birthday cake, topped with thick almond paste and lurid with pink icing. She presented this marvel to him at tea, and we all had to atone for his wan enthusiasm over it. He clearly could not wait to sink into his old leather chair in his study and review what Tocqueville had said about America. Needless to say, we were subjected to this discerning Frenchman for months thereafter, for now that my father actually possessed him for his own he could be more sure of the accuracy of quotations from him.

"It's extraordinary," he said one bitter Saturday evening in November when the wind from the Russian steppes and the North Sea was battering the parsonage, "that a young man just turned thirty could grasp as he did the essence and spirit of another country. Ansie, you can surely spare a moment from your stamps. I want all of you to listen to this:

In the United States the more opulent citizens take great care not to stand aloof from the people; on the contrary, they constantly keep on easy terms with the lower classes: they listen to them, they speak to them every day. They know that the rich in democracies always stand in need of the poor, and that in democratic times you attach a poor man to you more by your manner than by benefits conferred.

If you should care to memorize that really noble passage, Ansie—verbatim, mind you—I think I could dig up a sixpence as a reward."

"What about me?" I asked, sure that I had as good a memory as Ansie's, if not a better one.

"And me?" Mary echoed.

My father was so eager to rivet Tocqueville firmly upon our minds that he hesitated only for a moment, nor was he slow to seize an opportunity of furthering our acquaintance with him even at considerable cost.

"Very good," he said. "My offer holds. But why not vary the quotations? Here's another fine one:

I have seen no country in which Christianity is clothed with fewer forms, figures, and observances than in the United States, or where it presents more distinct, simple, and general notions to the mind.

And there's another noble statement in the Introduction to the whole work, which shows the religious nature of the author. I mean to use it as the chief part of my sermon on Sunday week. Just listen to this:

I am ignorant of God's designs, but I shall not cease to believe in them because I cannot fathom them, and I had rather mistrust my own capacity than His justice.

Why don't you girls choose those to win your sixpences? And remember, it's verbatim again and an excellent recital, or no rewards."

"Is that man always noble?" asked my mother a bit sharply, since with the early cold and the awful wind she had had an especially trying day.

"By no means," my father said, "but he always seems wise, at least to me. As a matter of fact, there are certain things about American democracy which he mistrusts; but in general he thinks it has a great deal to teach our older civilizations, and I must say I agree with him."

"I can easily see that," my mother answered as she folded her sewing and went toward the kitchen to prepare our tea. "It's just that nobility in large doses gets on my nerves."

With all my father's admiration for Tocqueville, he did not love him as he unquestionably loved Thoreau. His old copy of *Walden* was so thumbed and tattered from being carried in his pocket on a hundred fishing trips and another hundred solitary walks that we all determined on a fresh one for Christmas or another birthday. He thought Thoreau a greater man than Abraham Lincoln; indeed, he held not only that America had never produced his equal but that few if any other countries had done so.

"I'd rather see Walden Pond," he was fond of saying, "than even Delphi or the Roman Forum."

My mother always looked alarmed at this statement since she had learned that my father's wishes were not so much mere desires as they were prophecies awaiting only fulfillment.

He loved introducing Thoreau and especially *Walden* to rare bookish friends and acquaintances who were either hazy about the sage of Concord or quite ignorant of his independence, courage, wisdom, and faith. The vicar was among the ignorant.

One afternoon when Mr. Read had come for tea, my father repeated to him one of his favourite sentences from *Walden:*

I know of no more encouraging fact than the unquestionable ability of man to elevate his life by a conscious endeavour.

"My dear boy," asked the vicar, for to his seventy years my father still seemed young, "do you mean to tell me you really believe that?"

"I not only believe it, sir," said my father. "I stake my life on it, not to say my religion."

"Fancy that," the vicar said, looking a bit uncomfortable at the intrusion of religion. "Of course, it's pure Scripture, too, but I must say my long experience with human minds hasn't often borne it out. What else does this extraordinary fellow say?"

Then my father launched forth happily on Thoreau's retreat to Walden Pond to learn in solitude there what life had to teach him. The vicar listened courteously enough as my father quoted "lives of quiet desperation" which, according to Thoreau, most men live. He became hopelessly bewildered, however, when my father read to him the paragraph about the loss of "a hound, a bay horse, and a turtle dove."

"You wouldn't perhaps think that with all his wisdom, which I wouldn't for a moment disparage, this man was a bit of a zany?" he asked.

"The answer to that," my father said, "depends on just what you mean by a zany."

"Well, in other words, a crackbrain, at least in certain ways. That turtledove for instance. He doesn't even take the trouble to explain that dove."

"He had more sense, not to say more vision, than any man I've ever known," my father said, a trifle hotly, "in books or outside them."

In all his indignation and disappointment, however, he felt called upon to grant that Thoreau *had* been looked upon by many as at least uncommon in his way of life and thought; and the vicar, in his turn, felt relieved that he did not stand quite alone in his opinion.

"But isn't it just these uncommon men," my father persisted, "who have most to say to us? Isn't the Bible itself full of uncommon men?"

"That's undeniably true," the vicar admitted, "but, funnily enough perhaps, in everyday life they don't mix in so well."

"And yet," my father said, seeing that it was prudent to leave the realm of ideas for that of fact, "Thoreau was an extremely practical man as well. He gives here exactly what it cost him in American dollars and cents to live at Walden. He estimates that the total expense was twenty-seven and a half cents a week."

"What's that in English coinage?" asked the vicar.

"A shilling and twopence."

"Quite impossible," the vicar said, "unless, of course, his pond was full of fish and his woods of game."

"He came not to like hunting," my father said, determined to be honest about his idol, "but he did fish. He says Walden Pond was not very fertile in fish, and yet he names several kinds, especially pickerel, which, I take it, is an American variety of pike. There were perch, too, and bream, which are usually called shiners over there. In fact, he says a good bit about fishing in this book."

No information could have raised the status of Thoreau higher in the mind of the vicar; and my father, in view of this new approbation, took on added courage.

"He does say something about fishing in another sense. There's one place here where he says that the streams he mostly fished in were the streams of time and of the sky. What would you say to that, sir?"

The vicar's calm blue eyes became thoughtful then and even a little sad as though at threescore years and ten he feared that his own fishing had perhaps been too much circumscribed.

"I grant you that does take a bit of pondering on," he said. "I'll think on that."

When he started homeward he carried at his own request my father's sole copy of *Walden* under his long black cape. A fortnight later when my father went to the vicarage to reclaim his treasure he was unable to do so since the vicar had taken it on a solitary fishing expedition. We decided then not to wait for Christmas or a birthday, but to give him his present on just an ordinary day, which we straightway proceeded to do, to his amazement and even rapture.

13

My brother Ansie's discovery of the words on the Statue of Liberty coincided almost exactly with my father's final decision to emigrate to America. We had, of course, all known of the statue before, largely through my father's frequent references to it; but for some odd reason none of us had been made familiar with its inscription. Only a day after my father had left home in late February of 1901 to meet in London some mysterious American bishop of the Methodist Church, Ansie received a postcard from a visiting missionary who had heard him sing in our chapel and who was travelling about the

United States in the interests of darkest Africa. The Statue of Liberty itself was not on the card, which was given up entirely to the poem.

Ansie was so deeply impressed by its words (as had been kind, fumbling Mr. Grimes, our postman) that he had them all placed securely in his mind hours before my father's excited and exciting return that evening; in fact, he kept repeating them about the house and garden until all of us, including Katie, knew them almost as well as he did and were, I am afraid, growing somewhat weary of them merely from repetition:

> *Give me your tired, your poor,*
> *Your huddled masses yearning to breathe free,*
> *The wretched refuse of your teeming shore,*
> *Send these, the homeless, tempest-tossed, to me:*
> *I lift my lamp beside the golden door.*

Katie had her own reservations about the poem. After my mother had explained to her what *refuse* meant, that it was a noun and not a verb, she resented the idea that any English whatsoever were refuse. "Wretched refuse" only added to her resentment.

"Them Eye-talians, perhaps," she said, "an' maybe gypsies an' sechlike, but not proper English folk. An' us here breathes as free in this old land as in any new one. Us ain't homeless an' us ain't no poorer than the next. But say it to your father, Ansie. I can see it's his proper cuppa tea."

My mother agreed with Katie that the poem was precisely my father's cup of tea; and I think she rather dreaded the effect upon him of Ansie's impassioned recital of it once he had returned from London. I could see the words seething about in Ansie's mind as we all sat in my father's study on that fateful evening when the future loomed before us, not dark perhaps, but unknown and breath-taking. My father explained first of all what had happened in London. He spoke slowly and quietly as though he were thinking over each word as he uttered it.

This American bishop, who had heard of him from the seminary in Manchester and from other Wesleyan preachers in England, had urged him to accept a parish in New England, in a village known as Pepperell in the State of Maine. He might be called or sent elsewhere after a few years, the bishop said, since the Methodist Conferences in America encouraged moving about. Moreover, he might well rise far higher in a country where there was no Established Church, where, indeed, the Nonconformist sects were in the ascendancy. The word *chapel* was not used in America as it was in England, the bishop said. There all religious congregations were known as churches and looked upon quite as equals.

"Did you like this bishop?" my mother asked. She was darning an old red jersey of Ansie's, and the colour looked bright and warm in the lap of her grey dress.

"Very much," my father said, with only a momentary hesitation which was not lost upon my mother.

Then it became quiet in the study, for we were all busy with our thoughts. Curiosity, I could see, was deferring even Ansie's desire to recite his poem. A piece of smoking coal fell from the grate onto the hearthstone, and my father retrieved it with the fire tongs. My mother unwound a long strand of red wool from the ball in her lap, threaded her darning needle, and began to weave the strand in and out of the frayed elbow of the jersey. A sprig from the ivy on the wall of the house began to beat against the window in the rising wind.

"What's this place Pepperell like?" asked my sister Mary after a few minutes.

"A rather sizable village, I would say," my father said, "perhaps more like a town. This bishop said some two thousand people live there. It's in the eastern part of the State of Maine, not far from the Maritime Provinces. Those provinces belong to Canada and are under our own flag," he explained to us children.

"Maritime means the sea," Ansie said thoughtfully. "Would this village be on the seacoast, then?"

"Yes," my father said. "Men fish there as well as farm and, I gather, build boats in a small way. I grant the sea is a tempting idea. I've always thought I should like to live by the sea."

Mary and I were knitting scarves in bright bits of leftover wool for the summer sale of the Missionary Society; but now in our absorption in my father we stopped our work.

"Is there one of those academies in Pepperell?" I asked him.

"Yes. I found out about that. I told the bishop it was a matter of great moment—this question of a school for Ansie, and for my daughters too. He assured me that all the schools were good and that this academy made one ready for college without leaving home at all. I understand that this academy in Pepperell supplies an education for several other villages rather close at hand."

Then we were all silent again. Mary and I resumed our knitting. We could hear Katie moving about in the kitchen.

"I don't quite have a picture of this bishop," my mother said.

My father shifted his position in his big chair before he answered her.

"He's a big man," he said, "both tall and large, and very friendly in his ways. I would think he would be most able in managing matters, let us say, of a Conference. He's also very persuasive in his manner, I would say almost urgent." He paused. "He seems to think," he added, "that this is a call to me from God."

My mother, still busy with her weaving of the red wool,

did not speak for a few moments. Then she said:

"I'm always a bit skeptical myself about these calls from God."

None of us said anything. In the face of calls from God, the sea, an academy, fishing, and boatbuilding seemed matters too small to pursue.

My father drew his pipe from the pocket of his coat, but he did not fill or light it, only laid it on the table. Then he rose from his chair and stood by the fire. Although he was not an exceptionally tall man, he looked tall standing there. His thick dark hair, rather unruly like Ansie's and already greying at his temples, rose above his deeply lined forehead. His grey eyes were puzzled and even anxious as he looked upon us all. He had been holding some book as he talked about London and the bishop, and now he balanced it against his black waistcoat and placed his hands across it just as he always did in chapel.

"I think we should get this quite straight and clear in our minds," he said. "Your mother is quite right, as she usually is. I don't hold at all with this bishop about direct calls from God. God strengthens and sustains us all. We must never waver from that faith and knowledge. But I've never believed with some men in Church or chapel or among the Romanists that He devises special schemes and plans for men, or even tells them just what to do. His purposes, to my mind, are far higher than mere plans. I think instead that He has given us freedom to make our own decisions as to the way we lead our lives. He means for us to choose as best we know how, and then we pay whatever costs there may be from our own choices. There may, of course, have been these calls, these vocations, for certain gifted men. I wouldn't presume to say there haven't been, only I just don't think along those lines."

He stood by the fire, still holding the book against him. The coals in the grate glowed red and hot, and the sprig of ivy continued to tap and slap against the window.

"It's true that I've come to think of America as a land of promise," he continued. "Perhaps, in fact, I'm more than a bit silly in that thought. And yet I know we'll be giving up many things here that we love. We can't foresee what the costs may be if we decide to go. They might be heavy enough in many ways; but that's just the chance we have to take when we decide anything at all."

My mother's face brightened as she looked at him standing there; but she did not say anything. Nor did Mary and I, though Mary told me later that she couldn't help thinking of Moses or of Joshua leading us through the Red Sea or across the Jordan to our Promised Land. It was Ansie who broke the long silence.

"It might be very nice for you to rise higher," he said thoughtfully. "I'm sure we'd all be proud of that."

My father smiled at him, but made no reply.

"You'd miss Bury St. Edmunds, father," Ansie continued. "Not to go there would be one cost for you."

"Thank you for thinking of that, Ansie," my father said. "Yes, I should miss Bury sadly, I'm afraid."

"Still, I hope we shall go to America," Ansie said. "I'm sure we'd all be willing to help you pay any other costs there might be."

My mother's eyes filled suddenly with tears. She let the red jersey fall into her lap, and her ball of wool rolled to the floor. My father stooped to pick it up for her, and with that simple action the spell which had held us all seemed to break and allow us to be again in the familiar parsonage, ready for our evening tea.

"I think, Ansie," my mother said, her voice shaking a little, "that it's time now for you to say your poem."

"Poem?" asked my father, just as though he had never been

in London or met a bishop from America. "Poem? What poem?"

"Ansie will tell you," my mother said.

"I'd like to ask Katie in to hear it," said Ansie. "I think she'd like to."

"By all means ask Katie," my father said.

Katie looked pleased, if a bit flustered, when she came from the kitchen. She had hastily tied her white apron over her black dress and pinned her white cap on so quickly that one of its black ribbons in the back had got caught behind her left ear where it dangled across her cheek. My father offered her his chair; but she declined that honour, preferring to remain standing by the door. She whispered something to Ansie before my father went back to his chair and just before Ansie took his place to stand in front of the fire.

"Katie thinks I should explain first about the Statue of Liberty before I say the poem," Ansie said, "just in case I might possibly be asked to recite it in school."

"Very good," my father said.

Then Ansie began his prefatory speech. His eyes were shining as they shone in chapel and his yellow hair, unconfined by soapy water as on Sundays, was rumpled and untidy. He smiled at my mother as he took his place by the fire as though he and she already felt sure of my father's surprise and pleasure.

"The Statue of Liberty," he said, spacing his words carefully and making each round and clear, "is on an island in the harbour of New York City. Ships which bring strangers to America are bound to pass near it so that all can see it. It is over three hundred feet high, and it is made of a woman holding a torch high in her hand. She is the symbol of liberty to all these strangers. Her head is so large that forty people can stand inside it. This statue was given to the people of America by the people of France. It was placed in New York harbour in the year 1886. I hope someday to see this Statue of Liberty. There is a poem printed on the pedestal of the statue. This is the poem."

We all listened carefully as Ansie recited the poem. He took great pains with its every word. Katie stood in the doorway, her round face flushed with pride and wonder. She forgot all the indignation she had felt in the morning about the *refuse*. I knew then that she loved Ansie more than any other one of us.

When Ansie had finished, my father said:

"If you are willing, Ansie, I'm sure we should all like to hear the poem again."

Ansie was quite willing. His second rendering was even more fraught with excitement and meaning than the first had been. Katie did not stay for the second recital. She had left her handkerchief in the kitchen and was obliged to use her apron to wipe her eyes and to blow her nose.

14

Katie did not shed a tear, however, when she came to Southampton with our Suffolk grandparents to see us all embark for America. My mother was vastly proud of her, for she knew that Katie had been steeling herself for weeks to be stalwart and even gay over our departure. My father was proud of her, too, and grateful as well, for upon her own suggestion she was now to live with his mother and father and see that all went right with them. To leave them behind was a mighty wrench for him, perhaps the heaviest among those costs of our decision to emigrate, although they themselves had been eager and even urgent that he should go. Like Ansie they were proud in the thought that he might "rise higher" in a land where chapel was every whit as respectable as Church.

My grandfather, though nearing eighty, was still strong and straight in spite of years of Suffolk wind and mud; and my grandmother, only a little younger, seemed anything but frail and old. They had all manner of plans for their land and gardens which Katie would now help to make possible. We were never to give them so much as one anxious thought. And who could tell, my grandmother said, with life being as unpredictable as it was and surprises around every corner of it, that they might not be boarding a ship themselves before too long to come to visit us?

I knew I should always remember them standing there on the bustling, noisy, misty pier among other old parents, voicing without doubt similar cheerful myths. Katie stood between them, short and solid in her shabby brown coat and her old tan straw hat, with a rakish bunch of red cherries just in front of its high crown. We had seen those cherries every Sunday for four years, which span of time, Katie had assured us, was but a fraction of their actual age. I knew, too, that I should sadly miss the cherries.

"I hope you'll come, Katie," Ansie said, just at that point in all leave-takings when nothing whatever remains to be said.

He stood in front of Katie in his black jacket and his broad white collar. He had his cricket bat in one hand and in the other a satchel of heavy grey wool which she had fashioned for him to stow away his special treasures, his coins and stamps, his marbles, and bits of rock from this place and that which he valued.

"There's travellin' folks an' waitin' folks, Ansie," Katie said. "I'm one o' them as waits. I'm for old lands, not new. Only six or seven years an' you'll be comin' back a young gentleman from one o' them respectable academies to go to your father's college at Cambridge. I'll be 'ere waitin' to keep you starched up an' stuck close to your books. An' don't you go plasterin' your hair down with too much soap, Ansie. For meself, I fancy it risin' up, natural like."

Our Yorkshire grandparents did not come to see us off. The archdeacon wrote my mother a letter which arrived on the day before our departure for Southampton. When Mr. Grimes had left it at the door, said goodbye and God bless you to us all in a rather tremulous voice and thanked Ansie for the Statue of Liberty poem, which was a farewell gift, my mother stuck the letter beneath the Royal Family, whom we had returned to the drawing-room wall. She was quite too flustered, she said, with packing all our boxes which were strewn about the floor to open it at the moment. She had quite enough on her mind what with finding a place for Tocqueville and Thoreau, both of whom my father had insisted must be easily accessible on the ship, instead of being sent on ahead with his other books, to be able to endure any more confusion. The letter stayed there all day, its unknown and perhaps menacing contents concealed beneath Queen Victoria and an almost unbelievable number of descendants grouped respectfully around her ornate chair.

My mother read it aloud to us after we had been well stayed by our evening tea in my father's dismantled study with the last of the long summer twilight darkening the garden. Although he was naturally consumed by distress, my grandfather Oldroyd wrote, certain most important, in fact imminent affairs in his diocese would prevent his journeying so far south to bid us Godspeed; but we must be assured that his prayers were always with us. All the tired lines left my mother's face as she folded the letter and smiled at my father.

"I'm beginning now to believe in the mercies of God," she said. "And just to prove what a really good wife I am to you,

I won't say another word about your carrying that wretched *Walden* in your pocket though it does sag your jacket."

My father laughed as he had not laughed for weeks; and Ansie ran to the kitchen to tell Katie the good tidings from Yorkshire.

THREE · *The Voyage*

WHENEVER we reviewed our voyage of ten days on the *Empress of Austria* as we often did not only in the weeks and months immediately following it, but in years afterwards, we always remembered the Plimsolls above every other feature. They blotted out all the other astonishments or at least effectively obscured them. It seemed a sacrilege that Mr. Plimsoll, moving constantly about among our motley fellow passengers in his worn black frock coat and his frayed felt shoes, could quench our wonder over the long succession of completely windless days when the sea was as still as some slow Suffolk stream, my father said, and the great ship cut through the silvery expanse of pale-green water with as little disturbance as a swan floating beneath the willows of the Lark at Bury St. Edmunds. Or that he and his incredible family could dull our sorrow when a drunken Rumanian wrung the neck of a canary which an old Bohemian woman had smuggled on board as her greatest treasure and which had enraged the Rumanian by perching on his shoulder as it darted and fluttered about the crowded deck. Or that our amazement over them all could minimize our horror when two young Italians drew knives against each other in a fight over a Greek girl, the magnet to most of the men in our quarters except, of course, to Mr. Plimsoll, who in a noble attempt to separate the Italians received such blows from them both that he was hurtled across the deck like some piece of worthless baggage, and not, I fear, to the deep regret of anyone.

My mother, who declared soon after our embarkation that the "huddled masses" in the Statue of Liberty poem could never again be any mystery to her, kept reminding us a dozen times during our memorable crossing of the Atlantic that, had we accepted the archdeacon's generous offer of funds, we should forevermore have been deprived of the Plimsolls. The archdeacon for purely social reasons, my father said, and therefore unimportant and extremely distasteful, if not abhorrent to him, had volubly objected to our travelling as steerage passengers. The very thought, he wrote, kept him from sleep by night and from peace of mind by day. If to travel first class were out of the question, we must at least manage second, which management he would be glad to make possible from his own slender purse. My mother, in a weak moment, might have accepted her father's proposal on the theory that families who had little or nothing to offer in terms of emotional and spiritual gifts should be allowed to contribute material necessities whatever motive prompted their willingness; but my father was invulnerable and perhaps even a bit shocked by her disconcerting realism. Not only was he determined to shoulder his own responsibilities, he said, but he also eagerly welcomed the opportunity to travel as an emigrant among his fellow men, regardless of their race or their colour or their poverty. They were all men of good hope seeking to better their lot in a new land. Why should he who shared their common lot and believed devoutly in their dignity and value as human souls accept or even expect greater comfort than they were able to obtain for themselves and their families?

Whether my father ever wavered in his infinite faith in human worth and aspiration, or upon occasion questioned his exalted idea of human personality, he carefully never divulged to us; and, so far as was possible for her, my mother kept her opinions to herself during our days at sea with some nine hundred other pilgrims bound, like us, for a more abundant life. Most of these had boarded the ship in Hamburg and generously represented several Southern European countries. Those who had embarked in Southampton were few in number and, to use a kindly and inclusive adjective, distinctly *different* in background. Whenever the din and confusion on our deck, which was at the stern of the ship and open to the sky, became unbearable or Mr. Plimsoll too fervent and ubiquitous, my father went to the tiny cabin which he shared with Ansie where he could sit on the edge of his narrow bunk, read his Thoreau, and meditate upon, or perhaps even recapture, his faith in that dignity and value of the human spirit under whatever guise these qualities seemed to be quite successfully concealing themselves on our steamship.

2

My mother said that the very presence of the Plimsolls was a mystery, for, had they all been on the dock in Southampton, we could never have avoided seeing them. Ansie grieved that Katie had not seen them, since he felt sure that the daily journal of our voyage which he was keeping to send to her could never do justice to them all or take the place of Katie's own startled observation. Our sensible conclusion, of course, was that they had been hustled on board early, once the embarkation officials had recovered from their surprise. At all events, when we had reached the crowded deck, there they all were, gathered at the rail, Mr. and Mrs. Plimsoll, three pairs of twins, one baby in a battered pram, a younger in its mother's arms, and the six other assorted Plimsolls who completed the family circle of sixteen in all, not to mention the obvious prophecy of a seventeenth to be fulfilled before many weeks had passed.

Although the Plimsolls claimed most of our thoughts and many of our hours on board ship in much the same manner as they seized the attention of everyone else from harassed stewards to derisive or infuriated passengers, they vanished completely from our knowledge once we had reached New York and departed on our separate ways. The vastness of the Dakotas toward which they were journeying to engage in missionary labour on the limitless prairies of those still-new states seemed to have absorbed them all, erased them, swallowed them up. My mother sent Mrs. Plimsoll a present for the forthcoming baby more out of curiosity than kindness, she admitted, but no news of its arrival ever reached us; nor did Moses Plimsoll, who was Ansie's age and had aroused Ansie's sympathy because of his lame leg and the tragic fate of his rabbit, ever reply to Ansie's postcards. Still we never forgot them all or the extraordinary mixture of emotions which they aroused within us.

They had their more practical uses, too, for during Mrs. Gowan's visits to us, whenever she was about to enter her Betsy Ross world and cause us confusion, she could usually be deterred if one of us offered quickly enough to tell her about the Plimsolls. They never ceased to entertain her. Moreover, in their amusing or their pathetic aspects, they tended helpfully to dim the resentment and even bitterness which she had felt with good reason toward all Methodists until she had met my father.

3

The Reverend Abraham Plimsoll was a Primitive Methodist parson from a small village on the coast of North Cornwall; and he richly possessed and exhibited all the extreme and sensational habits which had marked that sect for nearly a hundred years before his day. He was a tall man and almost unbelievably thin. He had thin, reddish hair, a drooping moustache of the same colour and thinness, and a sparse goatee which could not hide his receding chin. His eyes were pale blue and blazed beneath their reddish brows with an almost frightening fervour. His high cheekbones blazed, too, with flushes of bright red, which disturbed my mother, although perhaps they were merely the result of the fire that burned within him and of his perpetual and frenzied tearing about. He wore always a long frock coat which hung from his shoulders and flapped about his legs. Both the coat and the trousers beneath had once been black, but were now almost green from wear and age. Two buttons were missing from the coat probably because of Mr. Plimsoll's agitated twirling of them. These Mrs. Plimsoll planned to replace if ever she could salvage a few minutes from her constant knitting.

The name Abraham had been given to Mr. Plimsoll by his mother, who had, he told my father, received it in a trance as a direct command from God. This trance was of continual inspiration to him since it undeniably placed his mother among similarly gifted Biblical characters such as Elijah, Balaam, the apostle Paul, and the father of John the Baptist. My father's one contribution to Mr. Plimsoll's busy days aboard ship was his explanation that the word *Abraham* in Hebrew meant "the high father of a people," which, since Mr. Plimsoll knew no Hebrew, came to him not only as a pleasant surprise but as an added assurance of his mission in life; and my father was charitable enough not to suggest his own amused application of it only to the size of the immediate Plimsoll family.

In general Mr. Plimsoll suspected my father, his lack of missionary zeal, upon which Mr. Plimsoll had unwisely counted, his quiet faith in mankind, his dislike of "love feasts" and camp meetings, which were Mr. Plimsoll's meat

and drink, and, above all, his university training. To Mr.
Plimsoll's explosive evangelism any learning valued for its
own sake was but a stumbling block to the saving of souls.
The Lord, he insisted, had carefully chosen the unlettered
to carry His Gospel throughout the world; and he himself
took as great pride in his own humble origin as a Cornish
miner's son and his almost total lack of education as he took
in the fact that the Primitive Methodists had been founded
by a joiner and a potter, who were determined to preserve
the "original zeal" of the Methodist movement. Once he and
my father discovered, after several heated sessions on our first
days at sea, that their respective understandings of this
original zeal were quite contrary to each other and that
their ideas about John Wesley were different, not to say
disparate, they forbore further argument, Mr. Plimsoll with
unconcealed contempt, my father with intense relief.

There was, however, little relief for anyone travelling steerage on the *Empress of Austria* from Mr. Plimsoll's constant
presence. He was like some vulture flapping about among
us all. The confusion of language on the ship like that at
Babel or in Jerusalem on the day of Pentecost did not in the
least deter or discourage him. Once he had discovered the
possession of even a few words of English by any of his
many-tongued brethren on board he attached himself like a
leech to the possessor and began to unload upon his victim
all the terrifying tenets of his cramped and ugly theology.
In the early morning he gathered his family in a corner of the
deck to lead them in prayer and in the singing of revivalistic
hymns; at meals from the well-filled Plimsoll table in the
centre of our crowded, untidy dining-room, he enforced
upon us all unwilling thanksgiving for our tasteless food; at
sunset he again held devotions in the midst of his cowed,
submissive brood, delighted when the circle was increased in

circumference by those who from mere astonishment watched and listened. He delighted, too, in the persecutions which he willingly endured and which included not only scorn and derision but upon occasion unsavoury and well-placed missiles aimed at him in fury by various young unregenerates from southern climes. Perhaps his one annoying source of suffering came from two Roman priests who refused to talk with him and who calmly read their breviaries in the midst of the hubbub of the deck, their dark thin faces clothed in sardonic indifference.

My father said that Mr. Plimsoll almost equalled St. Paul in the number and nature of the indignities heaped upon him with the exception of shipwreck and imprisonment. Indeed, he narrowly escaped the latter fate when some outraged ship's officers, descending on the fifth day into our chaotic midst, warned him that unless he ceased from his rantings he might find himself placed in confinement well below the deck. This threat may have slightly modified his zeal, though not too noticeably, for doubtless he was aware, as were we all, that steamship officials during those years of mass emigration did not overly concern themselves with the human freight which on every voyage crammed their steerage quarters.

4

It was impossible to feel any emotion whatever about Mrs. Plimsoll, except perhaps a satiated wonder, since she herself betrayed not the slightest awareness of her peculiar situation in life. So far as one could gather from her manner, her behaviour, or her rare conversation, she felt neither pride in her husband nor embarrassment over his antics. She took charge of her many children, all of whom were clean and decently behaved, but without any visible vestige of affection or concern. She managed to hold her youngest in her arms and keep her two-year-old beside her in his pram, to attend to their needs, and to quiet their frequent wailings; but she did all these things as though she were attending to extraneous pieces of furniture. My mother wondered if she knew that her fifteenth child was clearly imminent, might, it seemed, arrive at any hour, but of that she gave no sign. At their long table in our close, ill-ventilated dining-room, where children screamed in a dozen languages and stewards in soiled white coats commanded and cursed, where my father's fellow men snatched greedily at food and raucous shouts of laughter mingled with unpleasant smells, she sat, silent and imperturbable, seeing to the wants of her family like some machine stocked with necessities and emitting each as needed or desired. She sang at family services in a high, true voice, but with no change of expression, if, indeed, her sharp, thin face could be said to have an expression. She simply sat among her family like some extra piece of luggage which has been filled with unnecessary pieces and brought along in the thought that its contents might someday prove useful. She was apparently neither in a daze nor, perhaps unhappily for her, in a dream; she did not invite pity or anxiety; she rarely smiled and seldom spoke; she was merely there.

She was a small woman with dark straight hair drawn neatly back and coiled in a severe knot. Her eyes were small, dark, and lustreless. She wore every day a neat grey dress, the skirt of which was covered by a wide black sateen apron with a capacious pocket. In this pocket she carried her knitting. This knitting was the one evidence of any animation about her except for a nervous twitching in her right cheek which made its skin quiver as a still pool quivers from the sudden impact of a stone. She literally never ceased from knitting except at mealtimes or when one of the two babies demanded that she free her hands for necessary services. She kept her needles clicking even while she was singing at devotions. Her sole output was socks, which was understandable considering the number of her children; and she was so quick that she could turn out a pair a day whatever the size. The colour of these was of no importance at all to her. She had clearly never wasted a strand of wool since she had begun to knit. When one colour from the odds and ends in her pocket gave out, she simply used any other which came to her hand so that her finished products, at least, were gay and lively.

My mother, when she was finally convinced that Mrs. Plimsoll welcomed neither sympathy nor any form of assistance, was absorbed by curiosity concerning her and used her knitting as a means of satisfying this. When she had gotten together a quite generous supply of wool from our luggage in the cabin which she shared with Mary and me, she took it to Mrs. Plimsoll in the hope of engaging her in conversation. The conversation, however, was a disappointment. Beyond thanking my mother for the wool, Mrs. Plimsoll said nothing at all except, in rather a defensive way, that she did plan to restore Mr. Plimsoll's missing buttons once she could take time from her socks.

5

The fourteen Plimsoll children, who could not fail to appeal to our imaginations as to just what might prove to be their mission in the Dakotas except to provide a ready-made Sunday school there, were all named from the Old Testament. This fact, in turn, engrossed my father's curiosity, for, given Mr. Plimsoll's mania for spreading the Gospel, it seemed odd that he had bestowed upon his children Hebraic rather than Christian names. Since an impassable gulf had early separated him and my father, there seemed no way to solve this mystery; and my father had to content himself with the assumption that somewhere deep within Mr. Plimsoll's attenuated frame there glowed passionate memories of the patriarchs fleeing from false gods to pitch their tents in a forbidding land; or of Moses before the Burning Bush; or of the fury of Elijah by the river Kishon; or of the unspeakable sins of Sodom and Gomorrah. Or perhaps he was merely recognizing the ancient promise made to the original Abraham that his seed should be as the stars in number.

The Plimsoll family began with twin sons, Adam and Amos, who were tall, sober boys of fifteen. Two more pairs of twins followed them after the single births of Asenath, who was fourteen, and Rebekkah, who was twelve. Elijah and Elisha were eleven, Isaiah and Isaac nine, and in between came Moses, who was an undersized, pale little boy with puzzled, frightened eyes and a crutch, for he was lame from a shrunken leg. Below the latest twins were five other small Plimsolls ranging in age from eight to one. Each pair of twins was of the identical variety so far as one could determine; and all the fourteen, ten of whom were boys, resembled their father in features and colouring except Moses, who was like none of his brothers or sisters and totally unlike either parent. Mrs. Plimsoll had bequeathed nothing of her own appearance to any of her children. Indeed she seemed as nonexistent in them as in herself.

It was difficult to discover what the Plimsoll sons thought or felt about their father or just what they were actually like in themselves. In the intervals between their revivalistic services they wandered around the crowded deck usually in pairs and almost always silent. Adam and Amos were invariably kind to Moses, whom they often carried between them in a sort of sling made of a square of canvas gathered at two sides; and the eleven-year-old twins occasionally shared this responsibility. My mother was delighted one morning to see Elijah and Elisha engaged in a wrestling match, umpired by their older brothers. The match, however, could hardly be termed exciting and came to an abrupt close as soon as other boys on board who had gathered to see the fun began in a medley of tongues and a series of rough gestures to instruct the wrestlers in more violent tactics than they were clearly in the habit of employing against each other.

The Plimsoll daughters, Asenath and Rebekkah, were more loquacious and sociable than their brothers. They also offered more to their father, for they were either willing or eager to shout ejaculations in the family hymn singing and at intervals during his exhortations. "Glory, hallelujah!" Asenath would cry, and Rebekkah in obedience to a signal from her sister would add somewhat less stridently her "Amen" or "Jesus saves." They often attached themselves to Mary and me, perhaps out of genuine loneliness or the bond of a common language, or perhaps from curiosity in us as Methodists of a different sort from themselves. Asenath in particular concerned herself with the state of our souls; but when she discovered that such concern only made Mary nervous and tearful and me rude and stubborn, she contented herself with the story of her own and Rebekkah's conversion at a Cornish camp meeting, at which, we gathered, most of the Plimsolls above the age of nine had been likewise redeemed.

In the afternoons when many of our fellow travellers were sleeping in their bunks below or stretched out snoring in the sun and it was possible to find a clear space on the deck, my mother read aloud to us for an hour. Moses Plimsoll at Ansie's invitation joined us from the beginning; and after a few days the others of the flock, except the youngest who kept close to their impassive mother, came also. Adam and Amos perched self-consciously on the outside of the circle on the folding canvas chairs provided us in the steerage and stared at my mother as though she were some creature from another planet. Asenath and Rebekkah sat on their chairs also and knitted almost as swiftly and skillfully as their mother. The younger twins drew nearer day by day, sitting on the ends of their bony spines on the deck flooring and hugging their thin knees above their multicoloured socks. On the second day my mother impulsively took Moses on her lap, a place which, once he had recovered from his astonishment, gave him both pride and pleasure and which he shyly expected and claimed on all following days. If Mrs. Plimsoll, knitting on the opposite side of the deck and attending desultorily to the needs of her five youngest, observed him, she gave no sign; and his father was too immersed in his Bible or too agitated over the many sinners among us to pay the slightest attention to our occupation.

I think the Plimsolls really enjoyed our reading hours as the fine weather miraculously held and the ship moved onward over the calm sea in the hot sunshine. None of them, to be sure, was so entranced as Moses, whose big brown eyes began to lose their fear and to glow with delight and wonder; but even Adam and Amos brightened occasionally, and the younger twins rocked back and forth on the hard deck boards with excitement. *The Jungle Book* was obviously a new world to them all: Mowgli and his foster parents, the Wolves; the valiant mongoose, Rikki-tikki-tavi; Toomai and his elephant, Kala Nag.

My mother, her curiosity about them all still prodding her, used her reading as a means of appeasing it; and in this she was ably seconded by Ansie, who sought more material for his journal to Katie.

"Doesn't your mother read to you?" he asked one day, addressing this question to any Plimsoll who might be disposed to answer him.

"She don't have time," Rebekkah said.

"And if she did," Asenath added sharply, "she wouldn't read heathen books like that one. She'd read the Bible."

"Shut up, Asenath," Isaiah Plimsoll said, to my mother's relief and amazement.

"We read the Bible, too," Mary said, with more than a trace of anger in her voice.

Asenath clicked her needles furiously after darting a vengeful glance at Isaiah and a scornful one toward Mary. Ansie attempted to lighten the atmosphere.

"I don't think there are cobras like Nag and Nagaina on the prairies in America," he said, "but I'm sure there are rattlesnakes. They don't live in New England, where we are going, but they do in the Dakotas. My father has told me about them. You hold their heads down with a forked stick, and then you beat them to death."

"I hope I don't ever see one," Moses said with a shiver of fear.

"They mean to warn you in time," Ansie said with scant comfort. "They have rattles on their tails to warn you with."

"We'll take care of you, Moses," Amos said quickly. "Don't you go to worrying. We'll see that you don't see no snakes."

"God will protect us all," Asenath said with unctuous and repulsive piety. "We're going to do His work way out there, and He'll look out for us." She looked up from her knitting to shoot a mean glance at Moses. "Only maybe not you, Moses, to pay you for disobeying father about your rabbit."

"Leave him alone, Asenath," Adam said. "Keep your mouth shut!"

My mother, seeing that Mary was about to pounce upon

Asenath with a hot flow of words and that I was ready to lend her any amount of assistance, hastily swung the conversation to more general information.

"What town are you going to live in?" she asked the family at large.

The boys left the reply to their sisters, and since Asenath was sulky over Adam's rebuff, Rebekkah answered.

"In a place near Fargo in the State of North Dakota," she said. "I don't remember its name. Does anyone remember?"

Apparently no one did; but my mother, encouraged, continued her questions.

"What will you do there? I mean, will your father preach in a chapel of his own?"

"No," Asenath said, now sufficiently recovered to take on her position as spokesman for the family. "He'll hold camp meetings on the prairie for hundreds and hundreds of people who don't know nothing about Jesus. He'll ride a horse miles and miles; and we four oldest will likely ride horses too. In just a few more years," she finished proudly, "I shall be a missionary on my own. My father says so. I've had a call to preach the Gospel, and Rebekkah may have one, too, when she's as old as me."

Rebekkah had the grace to look at that moment as though such a call would be most unwelcome to her; and we warmed a bit toward her and toward each pair of twins as we sensed their combined filial hatred of Asenath.

6

My father never joined our reading circles. He confided to my mother that the very sight and sound of the Plimsolls was unnerving to him and that any closer contact with them would be devastating. Whenever he was on the deck he spent most of his time standing in the farthest corner of the stern and watching the shining swells of the ship's wake roll together until they again quieted into the flat expanse of still water. My mother felt anxious about him, for she feared that his thoughts were tumultuous and troubling. She was pleased when he occasionally talked with a rabbi, who had come from Warsaw and was going to New York to make his home with his son, a tailor there.

This rabbi was a frail old man with a long white beard, a sharp nose, and great, sorrowful dark eyes. He wore a small black skullcap on his bald head and even on the warmest days wrapped himself in the folds of a black shawl. He was very learned, my father said, and had borne many sufferings for the sake of his faith. He seemed completely unaware of the hubbub and uproar which surged about him. He sat in the midst of it all as though he dwelt in some closely encompassing world of sacred scrolls and the holy utterances of prophets and the ancient griefs of all mankind. Almost no one spoke to him although he knew many languages; yet all, even the most uncouth among us, felt an awed respect for him sitting there on the low roof of our main companionway, strangely alive in his own Realities. Whenever my father drew near to sit down beside him, he raised his right hand from his black shawl and said: "*Shalom*, my brother."

Although my father deplored all the Plimsolls except Moses and, after his initial arguments with Mr. Plimsoll, kept his distance from them in so far as it was possible to keep one's distance from anything or anybody in the steerage of the *Empress of Austria*, he was not in the least averse to hearing about them. As soon as Ansie at his request had gotten all their names from Moses and copied them for him on a sheet of paper, he went one afternoon to his cabin and amused himself for fully an hour by making them fit into classical metre. My mother said that if there were ever a perfect instance of a collision of worlds, it was exemplified by the Plimsolls, on the one hand, and Latin hexameters, on the other; but my father was proud of his accomplishment, which we all memorized and which remained in our minds long after the Dakotas had engulfed the Plimsolls:

> Adam, Asenath, Isaiah; Isaac, Rebekkah, Elijah.
> Amos, Naomi, Ruth, Seth; Aaron, Elisha, Job, Moses.

When later I began to scan my Vergil, the names of the fourteen Plimsolls were forever ousting those of Aeneas and Dido, old Anchises, and young Ascanius from the pages.

7

Moses Plimsoll called his rabbit Brownie. It was a baby rabbit, which his brother Amos had caught perhaps unwisely on some Cornish moor or heath and given to Moses only a short time before their departure for America. Moses had never before had a pet of his own. Since he could not bear to leave it behind, he had somehow managed to bring it with him, whether or not with the connivance and assistance of Amos we were never able to learn, but surely with neither the knowledge nor the approval of his father. Brownie was not born to thrive in any sort of captivity, and that of a stuffy berth on the *Empress of Austria* did not encourage its slender chance of life.

Moses kept his rabbit in a box at the foot of his bunk, which with fifteen other identical ones in a long row formed the sleeping quarters of the Plimsolls, quarters far less comfortable than ours and situated two decks lower down and well below the water line. Brownie cowered and quivered in his box for most of the day, though Moses and Ansie did their utmost at frequent intervals to make him hop about the bunk or nibble at some sorry vegetables which they managed to salvage at mealtimes. At night Moses held him close, in his arms, beneath his blanket.

Sometimes Ansie fetched him from Moses' bunk and carried him in his box to his and my father's cabin where there was more light and air, but he did not improve noticeably in activity; and Moses never ventured to take him to the open deck where both he and Brownie would be bound to suffer the venom of Asenath and likely as well to incur the pious wrath of his father. Moses felt sure that, once they had reached the Dakotas, his pet would flourish in an environment not unlike his native one, wax fat and merry; and Ansie carefully refrained from any further mention of rattlesnakes, which, he had rightly gathered, were able and eager to swallow rabbits as small and apathetic as was Brownie.

The struggle for Brownie's fragile existence was in vain. On the fifth morning at sea Moses awoke to find him motionless and quite stiff in his arms. When Adam and Amos, who went each morning to get Moses ready for breakfast, discovered what had happened, they did their utmost to dispose of Brownie after the manner of all worthless things aboard a ship and to accomplish this without the knowledge of the rest of the family or of the steward in charge of their location. That hard-faced German, however, appearing suddenly upon the scene, was so overcome by pity for Moses that he impulsively parted with his own penknife together with a dozen assorted picture postcards of the city of Berlin in an effort to make things more bearable for him. For in spite of the fact that after years of a thankless job he, like most stewards, cherished little sentiment toward human freight in general, he had been genuinely stirred by the thought of a child like Moses in the inescapable midst of the Plimsolls and had purposely made himself blind to Brownie's forbidden presence.

Ansie worried because Moses did not cry as he himself would have done over a similar loss; but apparently tears were a weakness neither encouraged nor assuaged by the Plimsolls. Moses merely looked more puzzled and frightened than before, as though this latest offering of life were quite beyond his comprehension, even if in keeping with his brief experience. My mother held him more closely now during our reading time, and my father often gave up his books or his staring at the sea to play draughts or dominoes with him and Ansie. We all waited and hoped for the look in his eyes to become once again less questioning and fearful; but in that we were disappointed.

8

Anxious as my mother was over the effects which, she feared, our passage might have upon my father's peace of mind and his ways of life and thought, she was troubled, too, about us children and especially perhaps over Ansie and me, whose knowledge of human experience, hitherto discreetly limited, had been suddenly and immeasurably widened and deepened by the unfamiliar sights and sounds on board ship. Our somewhat dim memories of stays on the Suffolk farm or those common occurrences in animal behaviour which surround all country children had heretofore made small impression upon us and had never been translated in our imaginations into human terms. Now on the teeming deck where people swarmed about in the sun we could hardly fail to become acutely aware of passions and greeds, desires and ferments, the existence of which we had never realized in our circumscribed decade of life. The Greek girl who shamelessly bared her breasts and offered her full lips to any one of a dozen men struggling to lie beside her; the half-clad children who were reluctant to go below decks when the trough by the rail offered a convenient toilet; mothers nursing babies in any available spot; boys and even men scrambling like so many dogs after fruit and confections which from time to time were thrown down by first-class passengers from the decks far above; fights and cursings, overlong pulls at jugs and bottles, blows and consequent yells, throwing of dice and of filthy cards, drunkenness, stupors, and snorings; the despair and discomfort of the old carried along by their families like extra and unwanted bales and boxes, or journeying alone to join sons and daughters in a strange new world—all these stamped their rude marks upon our minds. Mary, wiser in the ways of the world than we and at nearing thirteen far more sensitive to human conduct at its worst, was swept by such disgust and loathing that she often resorted to tears whereas we were consumed largely by surprise and shocked curiosity.

My father characteristically left all necessary explanations to my mother; and she was hampered by that reticence common to most mothers fifty years ago whatever their background or training, and especially to English ones. Nor was she able to glean much commiseration and understanding from other outraged women of her own land and language. For few of those who had boarded the ship at Southampton, except for the Plimsolls and a smattering of northern farmers bound for the wheat fields of Canada, had shared my father's desire for any close association with all sorts and conditions of men. Most of them were instead decently housed in second-class quarters and thus far removed from our maelstrom.

"See that steward kicking that girl lying on the deck," Ansie said. "Why does he do that? Men don't kick women and girls."

"I hope he kicks her some more," Mary said. "She's horrid

and filthy. I hate her. I hate everybody on this ship. I hate all the horrid men and all the dirty babies, and I hate Asenath Plimsoll worst of all. I wish we were all back home."

"Well, we're not," my mother said. "We're right here together, and there are only three days more. We'll forget all these unpleasant things before very long."

"I shall never forget them," Mary said. "Never, all my life." Ansie returned to his question.

"Why does he kick her like that?" he asked my mother.

"I suppose because he wants her to get up."

"Why is she always lying down like that?"

"Ask your father. He knows as well as I do."

"I did ask him. He said he didn't know. I asked him why she let all those men kiss her. He doesn't know that either."

"If he doesn't know, why do you expect me to?"

"Because you're always better at answers than he is. Besides, he's all shut up in his own thoughts."

"I'm afraid he's disappointed," my mother said. "I'm afraid all these people are different from what he hoped they'd be."

"He told me last night," Ansie said, "that we must believe America has better things for them. He said that perhaps right here on this ship there are future great musicians, like that Italian boy who plays his violin. He said you should never judge people just by what they look like and do when they are all crowded together like this. Do you believe that, too?"

"I suppose so," my mother said. "I suppose I *have* to believe it if I'm to go on living with your father. Why don't you fetch your marbles, Ansie, and show them to Moses? I'm sure he'd like seeing them. Or your stamps? Or your lead soldiers? Or—well, just anything!"

"Not me," Ansie said. "These kids grab things, and I

don't know how to tell them to give them back to me. Besides, Moses doesn't want to play. Adam said so. He's lying in his bunk, and it's smelly down there."

"You're not thinking of ever *not* living with father, are you?" I asked, for my mother's comment had struck fear to my heart in this world of arrant confusion.

"Don't be silly!" she said. "We're all of us getting too silly for words. We'll be just plain potty if we don't take care."

"Who wouldn't be potty on this crazy old ship?" Mary said. "Positively now, just who wouldn't?"

"Look!" Ansie whispered, his eyes big and shining. "That girl's running downstairs with that gypsy man chasing her. What's she going downstairs with him for? I'm going down and see what they're up to."

"You stay precisely where you are, Ansie," commanded my mother. "Why don't you say a poem for us or sing a hymn? You haven't sung once since we left Southampton."

"Frankly, Ansie, I'm sick and tired of you," Mary said. "You get more revolting by the hour. Why don't you go and sing with those odious Plimsolls? They're getting ready for another meeting right now."

Ansie looked as insulted as he felt.

"Do you think I'd sing those crazy hymns with them? I'm sorry for all those twins. They're not bad chaps. They're not like Asenath." He lowered his voice. "Their steward says Asenath is a filthy little bitch. Just what is a bitch, mother?"

"Ansie!" cried Mary. "Mother, make him stop using such words!"

My mother at that moment looked as though she were completely done for, crushed to bits, even her love for us all crumbling to nothing.

"Well, he did," Ansie persisted before she could recover

herself. "He said that very thing, and he called her a monster as well. He even thinks she may have sneaked to Moses' bunk and done something to Brownie to make him die sooner."

"Now, Ansie," my mother said, "that really will do for you. Asenath has quite enough sins against her as it is. She's not a murderer—at least not of rabbits. You can either say decent and pleasant things or else go straight to your cabin. And don't speak another word to that steward. If you do, I'll just have to consult your father."

"Here he comes now," Ansie said, chastened but by no means silenced. "They've driven him away from his place so that they can hold their horrid old meeting. Mrs. Plimsoll can hardly waddle, she's so fat. Do babies always make their mothers as fat as that?"

"Yes, they do," my mother said, watching my father weave his way toward us across the deck in his mussed old grey suit.

"Ansie!" cried Mary again. "You're only a child. You're not supposed to know about such things!"

"I know a lot more than you think I do, Miss Caxton," Ansie said loftily.

I drew near my mother and whispered in her ear.

"Were you big like that before Ansie and I were born?"

"Far bigger," my mother said gaily, as she put her arm around me and drew me close to her.

"Well, and how's my family?" my father asked, seizing an unoccupied camp stool and sitting down beside my mother.

"We're all fine," my mother said, though Mary was close to tears, and I was bewildered and unhappy, and Ansie was clearly the unrepentant culprit.

My father seemed unaware of any such convulsions among us.

"I can't get over the miracle of this weather," he said. "It demolishes all I've ever heard about an ocean crossing. Seven days and all fair and still! How fortunate we are! Fancy what it would be like if it were raining on this deck! I almost came to fetch you an hour ago, Ansie. There was a school of porpoises rolling in and out just beyond the stern."

"Why don't you have a few words with the old rabbi?" my mother suggested. "He's been sitting there quite alone all the morning long."

"That's precisely what I was aiming to do," my father said.

9

The fine weather changed on the day before we reached New York. There was neither rain nor wind, but instead a heavy, hot mist enveloped us, blotting out the sun and the sea, swathing us all in obscurity. Even the outlines of the steamship became invisible. No great stacks bellowing brown smoke upward, no broad upper decks where people laughed and loitered, not even rails and bulwarks could any longer be seen. We were as though on a mysterious phantom ship slipping alone and shapeless through some strange, dim realm of greyness and gloom. Our fellow travellers became vague, ghostly shadows, dark as they loomed near us, thin and pale as they vanished into distance.

Such a sunless dwelling place called for silence; but there was no silence. The wails of frightened children, lost in the thick, enfolding cloud, quavered and echoed through the motionless air. Shouts and curses and nervous laughter came from indistinct, hulking, colliding forms as they strove to find their way toward hidden doors and stairways or to discover those who had once belonged to them. The melancholy blast of the ship's foghorn was clamorous and constant.

An equally enveloping nameless dread seemed to be enclosing us all. This strange, smothering mist had in some indefinable way wrought a peculiar transformation in the very nature of all those embarked upon our common pilgrimage. A multitude of human beings, few of whom had enlisted sympathy or inspired respect among their companions, had suddenly become a host of helpless and forsaken souls, each uttering his own singular burden of sorrow.

In the afternoon, when the impenetrable haze still showed no signs of lightening and the boards of the deck were becoming wet and slippery, my father groped his way among the throngs of restless ghosts to help the rabbi to his berth below. When they emerged together from the mist and passed us huddled around my mother in a damp, silent half circle, we heard the old man say:

"It's like the darkness of Sheol or the black groves of Avernus; but there must be a golden branch among the shadows."

"What did he mean?" Ansie asked. "What's a golden branch among the shadows?"

"It's a talisman," my mother said. "It's a promise that all will come out right in the end."

10

Our motley collection of voyagers was curiously grave and silent during our last evening on the *Empress of Austria*. Perhaps the wraiths of fog, drifting below and dimming the lights in the dining-room, sobered them; perhaps their best clothes which all had donned for landing on the morrow made them self-conscious and uncommunicative; perhaps the nearness of an unknown land smote upon them with unanswerable questions and forebodings. From a noisy assemblage, bent on raucousness and crude manners, blatancy and clangor, they had become a company of anxious, homesick strangers. The many children, sensing the mood of their parents, were subdued, wondering, and diffident. Even the most voluble among the younger men and women said little, ate hastily, and left the long, untidy tables early to deal with the packing of their multifarious goods and chattels.

Mr. Plimsoll for the first time either forgot or forbore to ask a blessing for us all upon our food. Was he perchance finding his rampant faith wobbling, incompetent to deal with the practical necessities of the future? Or had he, perhaps, during that baffling, mist-hung day caught a fleeting glimpse of the sorrows of men, erasing for the moment, even in his taut and imprisoned mind, their many sins, their unrepentance, and their danger? His family surrounded him, restless within themselves, dumb, frightened. The quiver in Mrs. Plimsoll's cheek increased. For the first time we felt sorry for them all, not alone for Moses.

When we left our table, my father stopped for a moment at theirs.

"I want to wish you well, sir," he said to Mr. Plimsoll.

For an instant Mr. Plimsoll was too astounded to reply. One could see his amazement mounting within his old frock coat, upon which Mrs. Plimsoll had somehow managed to replace the missing buttons, until it reached his narrow, troubled eyes. Then he managed to rise from his chair above the clutter of the table. He extended his bony hand.

"And you, too . . . sir," he said to my father.

We went early to our cabins. Dank and dim as they were, they seemed a shelter from the still fog-enveloped deck or from our one inadequate, redolent common room. Moreover, my mother had our packing to do. She made Mary and me undress and climb into our narrow upper bunks under the low ceiling in order to be out of her way while, moving from my father's cabin to ours, she attempted to stow away our belongings in our many bags and boxes. She banished my father to the deck, but she allowed Ansie to collect his own belongings in the bag which Katie had made for him, warning him only to keep strictly out of her sight if he knew what was good for him.

Mary and I lay quiet in our bunks. I had the feeling that she was even more unhappy and homesick than I. The foghorn still sounded its long, mournful hootings, like the owls, I thought, in the spinney behind the parsonage or like the bellowings of the cattle, moving along the high-banked Suffolk roads toward the market at Bury St. Edmunds. Bury was at once a soothing and a sad memory. When, I wondered, should we ever go to Bury, my father and I eager for the abbey ruins, my mother, Mary, and Ansie wishing for Flatford Mill or for Ely, where at the Lamb Inn we always had tea and sugar cakes? On a tiny shelf above my bunk I had placed a few of my treasures. The little blue shoe was there, and I had a sudden impulse to hold it close in my hand. It was, I thought, my talisman, my golden branch among the shadows, my promise that all would come out right in the end.

I must have dropped off to sleep early in spite of my sad thoughts, for when I awoke the cabin was dark. Only the light from the curtained doorway showed a huge pile of luggage, strapped and ready, piled high on the extra lower berth. The ship seemed still. There was no racketing about as there had been on all the other nights. I could hear Mary and my mother whispering together below me; and I realized that Mary was in my mother's berth and that she was crying. I heard her ask: "Why does it all have to be so hateful and horrid?" and my mother say, "It's not really hateful and horrid. It's only new and strange. It will all be different when we have a home again."

"It won't be like our old home," Mary said.

"Yes, it will. We'll make it just the same, perhaps even better."

"How do you know we will? Maybe everyone is bad and sinful just as Asenath Plimsoll said. Maybe God punishes us all. How do we know He doesn't?"

"It's hard to know much of anything," my mother said. "I daresay we know just because your father knows so well." She laughed in the darkness. "Just think what it would be for us all if father were like Mr. Plimsoll!"

Mary managed a broken little laugh then, and I knew that things were better. After a few minutes I heard my mother say:

"Up you go, darling, for the very last night. In no time at all now we'll be having our own tea in our own new home and snuggling down in civilized beds."

We all three lay still, waiting for sleep and for the morning when, the steward had said, we should very early pass by the Statue of Liberty. I still held the tiny blue shoe in my hand.

Then all at once we heard Ansie singing. Perhaps he was making a kind of atonement for all his nagging and annoying questions or for his refusal to sing when my mother had asked him; or perhaps my father, for once discouraged and doubtful, had suggested it to him. Whatever the reason, his voice sounded through the open cabin doors and the thin partition just as it had sounded so many times before:

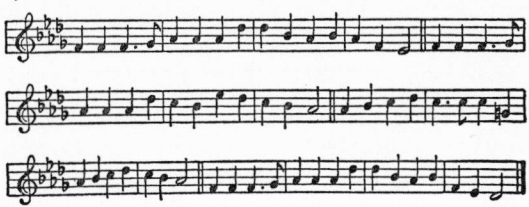

Through the night of doubt and sorrow
Onward goes the pilgrim band,
Singing songs of expectation,
Marching to the promised land.
Clear before us through the darkness
Gleams and burns the guiding light:
Brother clasps the hand of brother,
Stepping fearless through the night.

When he had finished, we all felt immeasurably more happy and safe. I knew that to Mary things did not seem quite so hateful and horrid and that my mother's stifled snifflings just below me came not from sadness, but from pride and pleasure.

Before we had finally drifted off to sleep, my father and Ansie drew our curtain suddenly aside, standing there together in relief against the light, their hair rumpled, their faces smiling.

"We thought we'd best tell the leader of this pilgrim band that the fog is lifting," my father said.

"And we pass the Statue of Liberty at six tomorrow," Ansie added.

"I haven't the faintest interest in that wretched statue," my mother said. "You boys get straight to bed."

FOUR · *Pepperell, Maine*

W_{HEN} I look back beyond these many years to our journey northward to Pepperell, I am still overcome by those first unimaginable wonders of a new land which fifty years of life in America have not been able to lessen or to dim. There were the initial astonishments of things themselves, their number, their variety, above all their length and breadth and height, their very bulk and magnitude. We were like Gulliver in Brobdingnag.

Huge, sweating black men bore our extra pieces of luggage through a mammoth, echoing station, not trundling them on a barrow, but burdened beneath them, on their shoulders, under their arms, in their hands. The locomotive which drew our incredibly high train was a shrieking monster, spouting smoke and flame, capable of consuming three of our tiny English steam engines which in comparison now seemed but snivelling weaklings. The great open coach in which we rode appalled my mother, accustomed as she was to the discreet enclosure of a railway carriage where, at most, eight silent passengers sat behind their newspapers. This long double line of dusty red-plush seats subjected us all to the curious scrutiny of a hundred pairs of eyes.

"You never told us American trains were like this," she said accusingly to my father.

"I didn't know myself," he answered, like some small

boy protesting at once both ignorance and innocence.

The magnitude and extent of the countryside itself amazed us once we had left the crowded confines of New York. Even the relative compactness of New England, when contrasted with western states unknown to us, seemed inconceivably vast and various to our alien eyes. The bright, sharply defined landscape constantly changed like some kaleidoscope. White villages slipped by, their houses made of wood instead of brick or plaster; white churches with steeples and gilded weather vanes; generous red or white barns, sometimes oddly attached to the houses by other white buildings, sometimes standing by themselves. We looked in vain for thatch.

"Do you think we shall have a barn in Pepperell?" Ansie asked. "I hope it will be red."

"Very likely," my father said. "Everyone here seems to have a barn."

He sat staring out the dirty window, which he had discovered to his discomfiture could not be raised or lowered by a strap. He was like a child who all the year has been looking forward to a rare orange in the toe of his Christmas stocking and, instead, has been overwhelmed by possessions unexpected and innumerable. Occasionally he reluctantly interrupted his gazing to consult a thick paper folder which named the cities and towns through which we were to pass.

"Does this train stop at a place called Concord?" he inquired of the burly, blue-clad conductor, who punched our long tickets.

"Which Concord?" the conductor asked. "There's one in Massachusetts, and there's another in New Hampshire."

"The one nearer Boston," my father said.

"They're neither of them on this run," the conductor said. He was clearly worried over us all. "You haven't made a mistake, have you? You wan't planning to go to Concord?"

"No," my father said. "At least not now. It's only that I have a friend who once lived there."

We went past fields, high fields, low rolling fields, ploughed fields given to garden produce, tall stalks of corn, harvested grain, a thousand fields beneath the blazing early September sun. No familiar hedges separated one from another, but, instead, fences of grey, interlocking logs or walls of piled grey stones. Sometimes brilliant red berries flamed against the stones. Now and then in a thicket a tree or a bush was crimson. The whole land, fields and thickets, valleys and hillsides, even the hollows beside the railroad tracks, were bordered or filled by the brilliant yellow plumes of some plant strange to us. Ansie's curiosity over all this prodigal splendour could not be curbed.

"Could you tell me what the yellow flowers are?" he asked a boy on one of his many trips to the water tank at the end of the car.

"Goldenrod," the boy said. "Ain't you ever seen goldenrod before? It's all over the place, come fall."

"It's goldenrod," Ansie said proudly, returning to his seat. "And the white and purple Michaelmas daisies, they call asters here. What's fall, father?"

"Fall?" asked my father. "Fall? Oh, I remember now. It's autumn. It's the American word for autumn. It means the falling of the year."

More falls of a different sort, falls of tumultuous water sliding over high dams by busy mills and factories. Waterfalls in the wide courses of rivers, which we thundered across on bridges or followed for miles past woods and farmlands. Tiny falls and swirling eddies in countless swift streams.

"American rivers are not much like the Little Ouse or the Stour," Mary said. Or the Lark, I thought, slipping beneath the abbot's ancient bridge, the drooping willows, and the limes at Bury.

"Many of these rivers have beautiful names," my father said. "Remember how we read about them in the encyclopedia? *Piscataqua, Androscoggin, Penobscot*, and *Kennebec?* I wish now I had found out their meanings in the Indian tongues, but I daresay we can learn those presently. Thoreau visited the Penobscot River about fifty years ago. He tells all about it in a book called *The Maine Woods*."

Pastures with rough outcroppings of ledges and grey boulders, pastures which seemed always to be climbing hills and then losing themselves in the transparent distance of the clear hot sky. Cattle edging their way among the rocks, staring stupidly at the train, or galloping off in panic at our uproar and our billowing smoke.

"There don't seem to be many sheep in New England," my father said.

Forests of dark trees, pines and firs and larches, and others strange to us. At times we hurtled through miles of such forests, thin white birches on their borders, a thick tangle of interlacing green beyond.

"It's easy to see why most houses in this country are made of wood," my mother said.

Numberless lakes and smaller ponds, reflecting the blue of the sky, sparkling beneath the sun. Small boats with fishermen as the day waned, their long poles sharp against the western light, their oars dipping in the cool water.

On the short coastline of New Hampshire, suddenly the sea with low islands far in the distance.

"The Isles of Shoals," the conductor said.

"I can't imagine anything shoal in this country," my mother said, wiping the soot and dust for the hundredth time from her streaming face.

"What's shoal?" Ansie asked.

"Shallow," my mother said.

Again the sea in Maine, waves rolling in to burst in white surf on long sandy beaches, the sails of ships against a far horizon, a white lighthouse on a rocky promontory. Miles of marshes with green and yellow grasses and thick reeds with sharp tops like spikes of brown felt. Tidal inlets making their way over pale, wrinkled mud, which was set with thousands of tiny blue and white shells. Hundreds of sea gulls, swooping in great circles through the air, resting on their wide grey wings, perching on poles rising here and there from the ooze, tracking through the slime and shallow water in search of food.

"The fens in the old days must have been much like these marshes," my father said.

Wider rivers, larger lakes, more white villages, fewer towns and cities, higher, rockier pastures, more small rushing streams, longer stretches of woodland. And always, until the night fell, the illimitable height and width of the sky, blue, cloudless, shimmering, looking even from the grimy windows of our coach as though it were boundless, far beyond the reach of human eyes, so vast that beneath it one felt unprotected and alone.

When in the darkness we changed trains for the last lap of our journey, this immensity of our new sky smote yet more intensely upon us. The sharp circumference, the unimpeded outlines of the moon, the brilliance of the constellations, the infinite number of the stars made us, as we gazed upward through the now cold air, incredulous, stunned. Here no low-hung clouds, no wandering wraiths of mist and fog, brought the moon closer to the earth or set the few visible stars almost on the tops of church towers or glittering among the very branches of the trees.

2

No foreigner coming to our shores, provided that his tastes are rural rather than urban, ever forgets or, indeed, quite recovers from his first experience of an American autumn. Especially is this true of the English countryman in whom is bred from infancy a passion for the land, for open air, interminable walks, a close and profound association with meadows and streams, animal life, trees, clouds, mist, rain, and soft sunlight. Autumn in England is lovely, to be sure—the green of summer, less vivid but lingering; the pale yellow of beeches and elms; the bronze of oaks; days likely to be windless; early twilights shadowy and still. Yet there the colouring, for the most part, is subdued and sombre: pale blues and greys of close skies, the fading brown of the hay ricks, the tans of cropped downs, the rusts of ploughed earth, the indifferent hues of the stubble fields. There is no blazonry on English hills; no ranks of trees in massed scarlet, gold, orange, and purple; no long succession of brilliant, diaphanous days; no New Jerusalem on every mean roadside.

Pepperell in September and throughout October overwhelmed us all. Its almost perfect half-moon of a harbour was enclosed by two high points of land, heavily wooded above their red cliffs with fir and spruce; but this growth was so interspersed with birch and beech trees that its darkness was fired by tongues of yellow flame. The rough fields above the rocky shore were tangled with red sumac and dense clusters of goldenrod, which glowed more brightly after the early light frosts. Behind the white houses along the main country road tumbled the pastures, purple, rose, and scarlet from great patches of blueberry, rising northward toward the hills which were clothed in like pageantry. In every marshy hollow the swamp maples were crimson; over every stone wall the red woodbine clambered; vast flocks of golden-winged birds hovered above the clumps of mountain ash, robbing them of their orange berries. The constant sun irradiated all, bathing the land with light, gleaming upon the full tide, heightening colours, lengthening shadows, silvering the wings of the gulls. As October ripened and waned, the sparkling air was filled with drifting leaves which, rustling downward, lay in roadside hollows and upon village lawns like open mines of gold and jewels. In the early evening after their work men raked these into piles for burning; and as the blue smoke curled upward and the piles were turned and scattered, the frail golden threads of ribs and stems glowed for a brief instant before they were consumed.

Autumn here in this new land had its sounds as well as its colours, sounds accentuated by the stillness and thinness of the atmosphere. The resonant trill and hum of millions of unseen insects filled the air by night as well as by day, not plaintive and intermittent like that of the hedge crickets at home, but shrill, high, buoyant, continuous. It was easy when walking among trees to hear the quick snap of leaves severed from boughs and twigs to float downward. Migrating birds in countless thousands flew overhead at dawn, twittering and crying, or, pausing for a brief space on their flight southward, chirped or sang all day as they foraged and scratched among the roadside growths. The calling of the gulls was clamorous; and the crazy laughter of the loons was repeated in high, tremulous echoes. Even the heavy, muffled sounds of labour, the thudding of mallets, the thumping of boards, the rattling of chains became more thin and clear as they resounded shoreward from the piers and slips where men worked at building small fishing or pleasure craft or from the open harbour when the fishing boats dropped their anchors.

3

My father in all this radiance of colour, this harmony of sound, now moved from strength to strength like those high-hearted pilgrims in the Psalm. Whatever unexpressed misgivings may have puzzled and tormented him as we crossed the Atlantic faded into nothingness. Hope rose again within him, strong and unassailable, that larger, all-encompassing hope inclusive of faith. The convictions and affirmations which since early manhood had shaped his thoughts and determined his manner of life became again steadfast and unshaken. Men were at heart again generous and kind, aware of their parts in the drama of existence, able and eager to play them nobly and well. Humanity moved ever onward, out of evil into good, out of ignorance and indifference toward wisdom and desire, sensible, however dimly, of the purposes of God. Without humanity thus created and endowed by Him, God could have no meaning, perhaps even no Being. All these thoughts, flooding his mind like a returning tide, seemed in this new freedom, under this high, limitless sky and among these bright hills, more invulnerable than they had ever been; and my mother, seeing him again both resilient and sure, confident, expectant, and content, looked herself more serene and happy than she had looked since we left Saintsbury, though I felt certain that she was more homesick than any of us for the old ways of England.

The meagre portion of humanity exemplified by the town, or perhaps more accurately the village of Pepperell, Maine, satisfied and reassured my father from the beginning of our sojourn. He felt secure and at home among men who laboured with their hands, believing as he did with the Apocryphal philosopher and poet that they, in truth, upheld "the fabric of the world." His impatient ardour to learn everything at once about his new environment amounted almost to voracity. He even seemed, to my mother's amusement, to be abandoning at least for the time being his Suffolk slowness and deliberation. He spent hours upon the small docks and wharves, asking eager questions about the building of boats, lending a hand at ordinary tasks. The intricate mysteries of weir-setting excited him as did the simpler framing of lobster traps and the constant mending of nets, spread out to dry upon the beach in the sun or on the grassy slopes above. He acquainted himself as well with the upland farming carried on not too prosperously above a rugged coastline given over largely to the various pursuits of seafaring. He sadly missed the presence of sheep and walked miles in order to discover a few on some distant hills. As to a lambing meadow, no one among either farmers or fishermen had ever so much as heard of such a phenomenon, which he took vast pleasure in describing to them.

He was almost equally engrossed in lesser matters: Mary's entrance into the academy, which was a red-brick building with a white-columned porch on a high hill above the harbour; Ansie's and mine into the grammar school, a battered wooden structure far less pretentious than the academy, on the country road a mile beyond the village centre; Ansie's new lore of baseball, and of football scrimmages, kicks, and passes. After tea, which we enjoyed a bit surreptitiously since it did not seem to be the general custom of the country, and before supper, Ansie initiated him into the batting of tosses in the field behind our house, both of them laughing at his good-humoured awkwardness, his almost complete ineptitude. The differences in the uses of words amused and charmed him. We children garnered these from our early days at school and sprang them upon him and my mother at meals.

"A boy at school ate too many crabapples and was terribly sick to his stomach," Ansie said.

My mother looked horrified.

"Ansie!" she said. "Kindly watch your language."

"I am," Ansie said. "They don't say just *sick* here. They say *to your stomach* as well. *Stomach* is a good American word. I wish I could say it to Katie or the vicar, or best of all, to Grandfather Oldroyd."

"They say *bug*, too," Mary contributed with a slight reminiscent shudder. "Bugs here are any insects at all, not just—you know what—as at home."

"Well, why not?" my father said. "Very graphic, I'm sure."

My mother looked unconvinced about the helpful vividness of *stomach* and *bug*, both unmentionable in decent English circles; but she added to our linguistic researches by telling how she had that day almost failed to buy a spool of thread in a village shop because she had asked for a *reel of cotton*.

"Incidentally, my dear," my father said, "you don't say *shop* here. *Shops* are *stores*, just as *cupboards* are *closets*, and *sweets* are *candy*, and *biscuits* are *crackers*, and *taps* are *faucets*."

He looked so pleased with himself that we forbore to tell him that we had discovered all these differences weeks ago.

4

Ansie got his red barn in Pepperell. It was not attached to the house as were several of our neighbours' barns, but instead stood well beyond it to the right behind our driveway and in front of our field. It had a spacious opening between two great doors to receive racks laden with hay in July, and, higher up, a smaller door for the pitching and stacking of the hay in its loft above the lower floor. On this lower floor there was room for three stalls, a grain bin, and an open space for carts and carriages. It was a generous barn, wide and relatively low, with a most agreeable roof slope. It looked snug and hospitable with its fresh red paint in honour of my father's arrival. Ansie loved it at sight, and, indeed, we all felt fortunate in its possession. In material comforts we were clearly far better cared for than the families of most Maine country parsons.

The barn and the parsonage itself had been bequeathed some ten years earlier to the church by a wifeless and childless Methodist deacon or elder. We were never quite sure of his exact identity, though we were grateful heirs to his bounty. "Whatever do you call these sidesmen, or wardens, or clerks in this odd church of yours?" my mother used to ask my father; but in spite of her frequent irritation over Methodism in general, she shared our pleasure in our new establishment. The parsonage was white with green shutters —or blinds, as we learned to say. Its rooms were large and sunny, and its furnishings, also bequeathed by the deacon or elder, were singularly free from eyesores like the Royal Family and Susannah Wesley. The Wesleys seemed, indeed, not to figure prominently in American Methodism, at least not in nomenclature. My father here in Pepperell was the Methodist minister, never the Wesleyan parson as at home.

Our lands, too, were generous. Behind the house and barn was a large, open field, which extended toward an equally large pasture, which in turn gave place to ample acreage of woodland. The field and the pasture were ours to use as we liked. Within a fortnight my father had bought a cow, an amiable, docile creature apparently of mixed parentage, since her dull-red sides, blotched liberally with white, marked no discernible inheritance. Her name was Lilla. At first we allowed her to roam in the field and feed well on the second growth of grass; but once my father discovered that Maine fields were sacred to hay and that pastures were the scantier portion of Maine cows, he moved her. He was excited daily over this unexpected mingling of small farming with his ministerial duties. His youth was returning, he said; but it would never be wholly with him again until he had a few sheep cropping around the pasture rocks with Lilla.

One of his parishioners, neither a deacon nor an elder, but merely the superintendent of the Sunday school, insisted on the loan of a horse since the nature of our parish in this land of vast distances demanded frequent drives into the outlying countryside. My father, overcome by such benevolence which, he said, exemplified all the Old Testament commands toward strangers together with half the New Testament parables, gladly welcomed an elderly yet adequate white mare named Snow White, complete with harness and a light carriage. With Lilla in one stall of our red barn and Snow White in another, he awaited only his sheep in our pasture for entire contentment.

My mother sorely missed a garden. In Maine there seemed to be no enclosures either behind or at one side of the houses and given to flowers, shrubs, and privacy. Instead, there were only neat lawns, punctuated by a few circular flower beds. A garden here meant a sizable plot of earth devoted to vegetables only and usually cut out from a field at close proximity to a house. Such was ours. We did have an orchard, however, which flanked our barn and nurtured a dozen hardy apple trees well laden with fruit. Ansie and I gathered the apples with great pride and stored them in barrels in our cool, dry cellar, also an innovation to us all.

5

The final bequest of the deacon or elder had been his housekeeper, who had not only cared for him during his declining years but for three Methodist preachers and their families preceding us. Her name was Mrs. Baxter. She was a permanent fixture of the parsonage, as much a part of it as a floor board, or the sitting-room fireplace, or its front door, or the invisible joists and timbers which framed it. She was not so much essential and necessary as she was inherent, intrinsic, and intact.

She was a widow of late middle age, in appearance solid rather than actually stout. She had very red cheeks, firm and smooth like Peggotty's in *David Copperfield*, discerning brown eyes, and steel-grey hair, so tautly drawn back from her forehead and ears into a tight pug at the exact centre of the back of her head that not one errant spear had any hope of escape or even momentary release. Her standards of exactness and perfection seemed almost awful to my mother, after Katie's easy, casual ways. Mrs. Baxter was by both conviction and inclination an enemy to anything casual. She was totally unable to understand those wholesome periods of indifference to mere detail which promise freedom and refreshment. Details were her sacraments. She yielded up her being with complete devotion to her spotless floors, her dustless tables and chairs, her folded, snowy sheets, her loaves of fragrant bread; and only after she and they had experienced full communion was she fully satisfied.

Inured as she had been for a decade to ministerial incumbents and their families, she had grown both sharp and sagacious in her summing up of human personality; and yet I am sure that our collective demands upon her discernment were costly at the beginning of our life together. My father was quite beyond her ken so far as Methodist parsons were known to her. She was puzzled by his courtesy and his quiet, slow ways. His absorbing pleasure and curiosity in his new parish at first startled and then delighted her. She was unused to such enthusiasm, such hourly interest and enlivenment. She was unused also to his apparent freedom from those niggling domestic anxieties which she had thought inescapable in the life of any rural parson. The quality which astonished her most, however, was his utter lack of domination both over his family and toward all church matters. This singular respect for the thoughts of others, even for those of us children and for her own (for he often came to 'her for information and advice), aroused at times uneasy speculations in her mind, first as to the manner of man he actually was and then as to whether or not he would be valued by his practical, hardheaded congregation. Perhaps these half-formed misgivings hastened her allegiance to him and prepared the way for what finally became her almost fierce protectiveness.

She was understandably chary toward my mother, cautious, perhaps at the start more than a little suspicious. The ministers' wives whom she had known were sobered and burdened by countless cares, borne nobly for the sake of their husbands. They had obviously expected no lives of their own. My mother's cares rested lightly upon her, or at all events gave that impression; she apparently had more life of her own than she could well manage and intended to preserve and enjoy it; and her treatment of my father often included a flippancy outside the range of Mrs. Baxter's imagination or of her former association with loyal Methodist helpmates. Nevertheless, although all her robust principles governing a woman's responsibility to her husband and home were constantly shattered by my mother, the fact that she was willing and eager to entrust Mrs. Baxter with the entire running of the household was not without its compensations. She grew slowly used to my mother's gay disregard of what to her were weighty decisions. Each morning they held a colloquy, revealing to them both, in the kitchen:

"What did you plan for supper, Mrs. Tillyard?"

"I didn't plan a thing. You always know. Do I need to plan?"

"Well, most women do around here. Perhaps they don't in England."

"Oh, I'm sure they do—that is, the really good ones."

"What I mean is, the other preachers' wives always did."

"I'm afraid I'm an utter failure as a preacher's wife, Mrs. Baxter, but possibly I might improve with time."

"I never said you was a failure. I only asked about supper."

"What is there at hand?"

"Well, there's baked beans to warm over, and applesauce, and I'd thought of some red-flannel hash as well."

"Do Maine people exist entirely on beans? Beans have been our 'meat day and night,' as the Psalmist says, ever since we came."

Mrs. Baxter winced perceptibly at this airy reference to the Psalms as well as at my mother's equally airy disposal of beans.

"Well, beans are cheap and filling, and I never want to throw away good nourishing food. Has the minister considered buying a pig? Most families around here keep a pig. There's a natural place under the barn for one, and pigs always pay their way, come time for killing. Reverend Perkins had two, and they kept us going all last winter in hams and pork and bacon, to say nothing of hogshead cheese, and the eating up of all the table scraps."

"Kindly forget a pig, Mrs. Baxter, for the moment. Just now my husband thinks of nothing but sheep."

"Sheep don't flourish in this part of Maine. Leastwise, almost no one keeps them. They get ticks."

"I don't know what ticks are, but tell him they're frightfully dangerous to human beings. Please don't forget."

"Where is he this fine morning?"

"He's fishing in the stream behind the pasture."

"Brook, we say here."

"Brook, then."

"Is he likely to bring home a string of trout in time for me to clean and fry them? They're always tasty and a real treat."

"Not a chance in the world. He took a book with him."

"Don't he ever go anywhere without a book?"

"Never, I'm afraid."

"Oh. Well, if you're sick and tired of beans, there's plenty of stuff for a nice red-flannel hash."

"Whatever do you mean by red-flannel hash? It sounds like a poultice."

"Good beets and potatoes and some leftover bits of meat. We Methodists favour it for church suppers, but the Baptists stick to beans and brown bread."

"I see. Red-flannel hash will do superbly. The children will have something new to write home about."

"You haven't forgot that you entertain the Ladies' League tomorrow afternoon, have you?"

"Alas, no! I wish I could. Whatever do we feed them?"

"I'd planned on cupcakes, plain and chocolate both. With tea, I suppose."

"Admirable! I'll make the tea. At least I know how to do that."

"You English drink a powerful lot of tea. Are you sure it's good for the children? Folks around here always think that too much tea is—well, binding to the bowels."

"It's never bound me. I've drunk it from six months old on, and I don't know anything that's made me feel more free. I hope I have a good cup or two on my deathbed."

Mrs. Baxter winced again at this irreverent mention of a solemn hour.

"The ladies really prefer coffee, but the cream's slack just now. The cow's not giving down too well. I tell your husband she's skittish from being in a new place. She'll calm down."

"I'm skittish, too, and I'm afraid I won't calm down. I'm going for a walk. I ought to stay inside and darn socks and write letters and help you in a dozen ways. But I can't—not with all this amazing colour."

"It *is* nice," Mrs. Baxter said, glancing through her clean and shining windows. "But I've seen it so often that I suppose I just take it for granted."

"Don't take anything for granted!" my mother called back from the open doorway. "It's fatal, and I mean just that. Fatal, Mrs. Baxter!"

Probably our new housekeeper took us children for granted far more easily than she was able to take our parents, who, although neither exerted any mastery over her, were her overseers, not to mention the added fact that my father was the present leader and custodian of her sturdy religious adherence. From the hour of our arrival Mary won her respect because of her tidy ways. Ansie and I, whom she looked upon as an inseparable team since we did most things together except when other boys claimed Ansie's time and interest, clambered more slowly into her good graces through our early dependence upon her in the matter of food. When we hurried home from school in the late afternoon, we always burst in the side door upon her faultless kitchen. For the first few days we hardly knew whether to be pleased or terrified to see her sitting there, by the window, in her red rocker, herself scrubbed like her yellow floor boards, her skirts covered by a starched white apron, her hands always busy at knitting or crochet, her eyes on the clock on the shelf above the sink, her nose carefully assessing her oven or her polished stewing pans, her hair in strict precision. But once she began putting out cookies and milk for us of her own free will without our so much as hinting at hunger, we knew that the game was won.

I understood from the beginning that she favoured Ansie over me just as all women, I was discovering, really preferred boys to girls, just as the faces of mothers were always more brightly illumined at the sight of sons rather than of daughters. Even Mrs. Baxter's firm red cheeks creased with pleasure whenever Ansie asked her for an extra cooky or a bit of twine, or sniffed expectantly around her gleaming stove. She proved a help to him with his arithmetic, which he fell into the habit of doing at her kitchen table in the evenings.

"Sorry, father," he would say, when we had all gathered in the sitting-room after supper, "but I'm afraid Mrs. Baxter is a bit better than you are at these queer problems. Do you mind awfully if I ask her?"

My mother always answered him before my father had gotten around to do so.

"Not in the least," she said. "Delighted, in fact. And don't forget to ask her—most politely, mind you—for our tea tray at nine o'clock. You can bring it in yourself."

Of Mrs. Baxter's further past we knew nothing, since, like all English people, we were shy of personal questions, and she did not evince any eagerness to enlighten us. She seemed to have been eternally involved with Methodist preachers. Reverend Hinckley, Reverend Wilson, Reverend Perkins, our forerunners in the parsonage, were but three among the many whom she had known and without doubt rigorously nurtured even though not under the inherited rooftree. Mr. Baxter had evidently died at a fairly early age. What his life had been like with Mrs. Baxter was, to my mother at least, a subject of amused conjecture.

6

My father's immediate pleasure in Pepperell extended to his church. This stood perhaps a quarter of a mile westward from the parsonage and on the opposite side of the rising country road. It was a dignified, even stately white church of the type often seen in old New England villages. It had four rounded white pillars at the entrance, a graceful steeple, green shutters, and high, clear windows, three on either side, through which the sunlight fell across its high-backed white pews. Behind it woods rose, green and still, and it was flanked by open fields. In every respect it was a church rather than a chapel.

From his researches into the ecclesiastical history of eastern Maine my father learned that the church had originally been of the Congregational denomination like the great majority of those Maine coast churches founded in the late eighteenth and early nineteenth centuries by stout Puritans from Massachusetts, of which Maine itself had been a northern province until 1820, when it became a state. He also gathered that among the various Protestant sects in Maine and, for that matter, throughout New England the Congregationalists from the time of the earliest settlements had held first place in social as well as in religious esteem. The Methodists and Baptists, who had appeared later in most communities and largely by way of itinerant or of lay missionaries, were in a distinctly subordinate position from the start and also of relatively inferior variety in matters of learning and in terms of cultural background.

Just where the descendants of the Congregational founders of our parish now were, whether their zeal had diminished or whether they had left Pepperell for wider and more gracious fields of activity, was never quite clear. If any of them remained among us, they were not voluble concerning their former doctrinal adherence or apparently dissatisfied with their present lot. Community memories, and loyalties as well, are destined, however sadly, to grow dim and uncertain during half a century. All that my father seemed able to discover was that the Methodists had superseded the Congregationalists some fifty years previously and most wisely had taken over their really beautiful church. And this wisdom was more strongly borne in upon him as he grew further acquainted with examples of purely Methodist architecture in neighbouring coast towns and villages.

The only other church in Pepperell besides our own was the Baptist church; and it was always called the Baptist meetinghouse instead of the Baptist church. Since this difference in terms was at first confusing to my father, who was aware of no visible social contrast between the two congregations and in his new freedom would have deplored any such distinction, he tried to discover the source of its widespread usage. There was none, the Baptist minister told him, except that of custom. For some reason, doubtless as unimportant as it was obscure, the Baptists favoured this name for their rather graceless, nondescript brown-shingled building which stood nearer the centre of the village than did ours. In quantity they were much the same as we; in quality, likewise. Indeed, it was difficult to detect any outstanding dissimilarities between our respective congregations except for the practice of immersion of converts in the cold water of the harbour which the Baptists strictly observed whatever the season, and, as my mother somewhat lightly added, their predilection for baked beans instead of red-flannel hash for their frequent church suppers. In general we typified two inconsequential country parishes, strongly Protestant by inheritance rather than by informed intelligence, uninclined to question matters of either doctrine or observance, each devoted by habit and tradition rather than by studied conviction to its own adherence, both struggling to obtain the means for a separate and decent existence, mildly competitive in social affairs and in public performances, covetous of new recruits only once a year. Our counterparts might have been found in a thousand other rural communities, similarly situated and as meagrely endowed.

Mr. Kimball was the Baptist minister, and like all other ministers in our region he was called Reverend Kimball, a title which was never granted any helpful article to lend it grace or dignity. He was an elderly man and had held his charge for years, since the Baptists, unlike the Methodists, tended toward permanence in the tenure of their pastors rather than toward frequent change. The most charitable estimate of him could not accord him more than a modicum of learning or any deep desire for increasing it. His theology was rigid and unyielding; but its terrors did not seem to cause him any personal alarm though he often gave fervent utterances to them from his pulpit. He was kind and cordial. In his hours free from pastoral duties, which he performed diligently and well, he dug clams, picked berries, and fished for flounders on the high tides in order to provide for his own table and, therefore, eke out his slender salary. Not infrequently he brought us some of the fruits of these avocations. His wife was a busy, tired, angular woman, who was famous locally for her unsurpassed cooking, for her good works, and for her cheerless willingness to perform all manner of parish duties unpalatable to others.

My father and Reverend Kimball did not discover many interests in common. Mr. Kimball's theology was so tightly done up and put away that it was difficult of easy access, unlike that of the vicar at home—which was probably, on the whole, fortunate. He did not care much for books in general, and he recognized no past beyond that of Pepperell and his long stay there. There were no discernible antiquities in Maine; my father preferred trout to flounder fishing; and Mr. Kimball, like most of the people in Pepperell, neither rode a bicycle nor was interested in ranging the countryside to observe its natural gifts. Nevertheless, they got on well together, forbearing with one another after the good advice of St. Paul; and if my father was puzzling to his fellow preacher, that in itself was not strange, my mother said, since he was still a puzzle to her after some fourteen years. Moreover, any whims or vagaries on his part which seemed odd and unorthodox to Mr. Kimball could be safely and even generously explained on the ground that he was a foreigner and, of course, as yet unacquainted with the ways of a new religious environment.

We all sadly missed the Church of England, at least in its outward and visible forms. It was difficult to accustom ourselves to the total absence of those square, grey-stone towers rising above clusters of trees and snug green church-yards, never to see in this new land Norman porches or fourteenth-century window tracery, never to smell that damp, musty, clinging smell of many centuries, never to hear peals of bells echoing for Evensong across quiet meadows and over slow streams. My mother unwillingly learned to call Anglican churches Episcopal; but the name itself was all she could possess of her early religious upbringing since only the larger towns and cities in Maine had any Episcopal church.

They were all out of her reach except by a considerable train journey even if, under the circumstances, she had felt it wise upon rare occasions to seek one out.

The Roman Catholics had no existence whatever at that time in rural Maine. They were all safely confined to the few distant industrial centres or to the French settlements well beyond the Canadian border. Needless to say, both their absence and their remoteness were sources of suspicious relief to a community so entirely Protestant as our own.

In short, the Methodist bishop had been quite accurate in what he had told my father. The State of Maine, New England, and the greater part of the United States as a whole were at the turn of the century almost entirely, in the English term, Nonconformist; and since America from the start had determined against an Established Church, from the very idea of which her founders had fled, she had no need in her religious vocabulary for the word *chapel* to designate any of her various sects.

Surely, no costs which my father was to pay for his decision to come to America were levied by his new religious environment. They could not be ascribed either to the Baptists or to his own Methodist congregation. Instead, they lurked, as such costs always lurk, within the fabric of his own nature, in that Fate which as the ancients well knew each man bears inescapably within himself "for good or for ill" and often for a mysterious and unfathomable entanglement of both.

7

During our first winter in Pepperell my mother occasionally observed that, in a country dedicated to the principle of nonconformity, we were in actual practice required to conform to more than a few distasteful customs. My father's cheerful reply to that observation was, first, that any arch-deacon's daughter who had been rash enough to marry a Wesleyan parson should not at this late date be overly dis-tressed by distasteful features in her recklessly chosen life, and, second, that in all honesty she should use the adjective to describe her own opinions since he was not aware of any incurably distasteful custom in his new parish. In general, he said, he saw as yet no reason to disagree with Alexis de Tocqueville in his praise of the simplicity which marked Christianity in America.

It was true that he and Mr. Kimball hardly saw eye to eye in church manners and methods; but he had met such divergence elsewhere and had no intention of conforming to habits not his own. It was even more true that the first week in January, known as the Week of Prayer and dedicated in Pepperell, as in many other Maine villages at that time, to the fervent recruiting by both churches of those who were outside their folds, did cause him more than a little distress because such covetous zeal was at variance with his own convictions, which held that, though all men were erring, none was irretrievably lost. Still, one week out of fifty-two meant only an infinitesimal percentage of vexation, especially since Mr. Kimball was only too happy to take precedence over my father in its ardent practices. And as it beneficently happened, a three days' snowfall at the beginning of that trying period helped immeasurably to tranquillize its annoy-ances.

None of us, accustomed to the brief and infrequent snow flurries and squalls of East Anglia, had ever before imagined such snow, coming in the midst of what was known in Maine as an "open winter," lying five feet deep in the valleys, softening the contours of the hills, etching the black trunks of the trees, enclosing all in profound white silence.